142 - "home inside yourself"
141 - words as "home" — ("... for gettin' hated in")
152 } "idea of home

7, 12, 14-5, 28 (naming the disease gives control)

CUCKOO

nest

words

CUCKOO

28

LINDA
ANDERSON

BRANDON

First published in paperback in 1988
Brandon Ireland & UK,
Cooleen, Dingle, Co. Kerry, Ireland

© Linda Anderson 1986

British Library Cataloguing in Publication Data

Anderson, Linda
    Cuckoo.
    I. Title
    823′.914[F]

    ISBN 0−86322−100−9

Thanks are due to the following for permission to quote copyright material:

Hamish Hamilton Ltd and Lyle Stuart Inc: Sartre, *Being and Nothingness*.
Penguin Books Ltd and The Viking Press: Arthur Miller, *After the Fall*, ©
    1964 by Arthur Miller.
Faber and Faber Ltd: T. S. Elliot, *The Hollow Men*.
Westminster Music Ltd: Joan Armatrading, *Somebody Who Loves You*.
Michael B. Yeats and Macmillan London: W. B. Yeats, *The Lake Isle of
    Innisfree*.
Harcourt Brace Jovanovich Inc. and The Women's Press: Alice Walker, *The
    Color Purple*.
Harold Ober Associates Inc: Zdena Berger, *Tell Me Another Morning*,
    published by Michael Joseph Ltd and Harper and Row.
David Higham Associates Ltd: Dylan Thomas, *Collected Poems*, published
    by J. M. Dent.

This book is published with the financial assistance of the Arts Council/An
Chomhairle Ealaíon, Ireland

Cover design: Design II
Printed by Billing & Sons Ltd, Worcester

TO DORY

'Love is dark but no stranger'
Joan Armatrading ←

1

The Still Point of the Turning World
May 1982

I have no use for people. That's what I told myself. No use. No need. No fool me. I would neither prey nor pray. Such puns delighted me. Pun-fun. I loved words, sometimes more than the things they try to represent. I loved. . .

Recently I almost loved a man. His name was Mark. Mark Time, I called him privately, because I was always waiting for him to call, to write, to be free to see me. He was a Married Man, but that didn't bother me. He talked copiously about his children, their dazzling school reports, vaccinations, illnesses, nightmares, clamourings for toys, money, and pets. In bed he talked about his wife freely and without spite.

'Your skin is warmer than Helen's.'

'Why do you shave under your arms? Helen wouldn't dream. . .'

'Your pubic hair is of a different texture.'

It was as if he were conducting a prolonged aesthetic and erotic trial, but without much detriment to the experimentees. Helen's friendly ghost always seemed to be half-hiding in the bedroom shadows. I didn't care. Marriage made my lover banal and that was my secret weapon against him.

But. . . One day he was driving me into the country for some pastoral coitus when an old woman emerged suddenly between hedgerows. She was waving at us to stop and looked ready to fling herself under the wheels. Mark braked and leapt out of the car to run over to her side. I climbed out clumsily, taking in the details of the woman. Tangled hair. Watery, beseeching eyes. Shawl draped round her shoulders and fastened with a safety pin. Slippers and men's socks. Mark's solicitous hand already pat-patting her shoulder. I don't know why but the sight of his hand touching that old woman gave me such physical distress, I almost laughed. For a moment I thought I would be sick and leaned against the car to steady myself.

'Is there an accident?' he was saying. 'Someone taken ill?' The

7

woman started squeezing his other hand.

'You mustn't believe anything you've heard about me,' she begged him. 'They've turned everyone against me. Lies, wicked lies. They say I spread germs, I've done something dreadful. They chase me all the time, never let me sleep. . .'

Mark blushed and scratched his neck. His style of conversation, which was always affirming, consolatory, and temperate, had failed him and he had no spare bag of tricks. I watched them for a few minutes, the helpless man and woman. Then I stepped up to them, released his philanthropic mitt finger by finger from her grip, all the while talking in a soapy nursey voice.

'Let's get you inside, out of sight, see? Then Mark and I will go straight to the police, tell them you're innocent. They'll catch the bad men and give them an injection to make them lose their memory. . .'

I led her like a tired stricken child into her dank shit-smelling hellhole of a house.

'Sit down,' I kept pleading, but she peered and poked around frantically.

'My bag, O God, where is my bag?'

I found it lying beside an old mattress on the floor. She started rooting through the jumble of contents.

'I'll give you money, as much as you like, anything, only stay here, stay. . .'

I sprinted back down the garden path. Mark was already in the car with the engine revving.

'OK?' he asked.

I nodded.

We sat in mute shame all the way back, partners in crime. It was over between us. We had strayed accidentally into a new field of force and it was over between us. I wanted to scream at him that he would never dare leave his wife. Never dare alter anything in his orderly hygienic universe. Even the inside of his head was law-abiding. I imagined squadrons of passionless mouse-grey thoughts trooping without hitch round his skull. I recalled without mercy the dull ticker tape of his speech. As I compiled my evidence against him, the woman's face kept interrupting like a pop-up monster in a children's book. Was she thinking about me? Turning me into an actor in her waking nightmare? Would her persecutors now wear my face? I didn't bargain for her becoming my persecutor. But for a long time afterwards she followed me into my dreams, trailing her stink. A witch. An Ancient

Marionette. She looked like the face of my future, loveless, penniless, tormentors whispering in my ear, demons tweaking at my flesh.

It was over between Mark and me but, according to custom, we went on for a while longer. He began to call me 'Darling' instead of my name. He talked to me softly, caressingly, touched me softly, regretfully, as if he were remembering me.

I sought revenge upon myself. I recall a lot of men climbing on and off. Plenty of fish in the sea, they say. Plenty of pebbles on the beach. Cold average fish. Hard average pebbles.

No one touched my heart, so I remained chaste.

One night after the usual copulatory contests, I flushed my supplies of contraceptive pills down the toilet. Then I danced round every room in my flat. In the next few months I discovered that my need for sex had been a superstition. Oblivion was what I was after and sex had been the route.

I couldn't stand my job any more. The journeys to and from the office. The zombie-march up and down the tube escalator. The ocean of bobbing heads in the streets. The hours of blank spiritless rage at the desk. I tried to cope by eradicating all feelings in myself except mockery and judgement. My job was to type letters of two categories. The grovelling sprinkled-with-compliments variety or terse smack-in-the-face jobs. (My boss talked a lot about 'superiors' and 'subordinates'.)

My other tasks were to file correspondence, take phone calls, and make him feel important. I shared the office with two women, Brenda and Daphne, who behaved with cringing niceness, all girlie voices and 'Yes certainly. . . Can I help you. . .' to their co-workers, whom they would later mimic and satirize with a venom occasionally spiked with wit.

They drank coffee in the morning, tea in the afternoon, every hour, on the hour. If I refused a drink, they would look huffy. If I switched on the kettle before the appointed time, they would blink and throw vexed looks at the clock, as if they felt the world tilt dangerously. For months they scoured magazines for advertisements inviting consumers to send off 'freepost' for more details. They inserted the boss's name and home address on the clip-out forms and giggled at the prospect of him being inundated with catalogues and circulars on computer dating, double glazing, deaf aids, toupees. It was their idea of sedition. Or humour. They were fanatical cat-lovers and had turned the office into a shrine adorned with soft-focus close-ups of cats with malicious intelligent eyes and glistening whiskers. The two women were always exchanging recondite formulae on how to eliminate odours of catpee and catsick from the home. They swapped stories about the latest adventures of their Corky, Sooty, Monty, Judy, and Topsy.

'Oh, isn't that swee. . .eet!' they would chorus. I used to ring the speaking clock or 'Dial-a-Recipe' and keep the receiver clamped to my ear so that I wouldn't hear them. On the morning before I never worked again, I was listening to instructions for Rice and Apple Bake, learning what to do with the cream and almonds ('ormonds' was how the voice pronounced it), when my boss slinked in on his soft sneaky soles.

'So sorry to disturb you,' he said. 'I never know whether you're free to serve me. Perhaps you should have a red light you could switch on when you're available.' Serve. Red light. Available.

'Why don't you go and fuck yourself?' I asked him discreetly.

There ensued protracted irritable sessions in the Personnel department. Flushed with magnanimity, my boss asserted that he would be only too ready to understand, to forgive, a momentary aberration, a mad impulse, out of character, a person of your background. . . As if I were some moneyed aristo drudging in an office to express my eccentricity. *amazing energy*

'I have daughters myself,' he went on, hint of a tear behind his thumb-smeared glasses. 'I know all about the time of the month and its attendant difficulties.'

'If crass behaviour is linked to the menstrual cycle,' I asked, 'how do you explain yours?'

When the money ran out and I had to survive on dole cheques, I moved out of my flat in an up-and-coming about-to-be-fashionable area and into a poky room in a Stoke Newington terraced house. The hallways smelt of cooking and poverty. My door was identical to all the others, except that some humourist had fixed a brass knocker in the shape of Shakespeare's head to the outside. I told myself not to mind, freedom has its price. And I like austere uncluttered space, no pictures, ornaments, and superfluous furniture to catch and snarl the attention. But in the communal bathroom there were hairs in the sink, puddles on the floor, intimate stains of anonymous neighbours in the toilet bowl. Best not to look, I decided. 'A whole new life is beginning,' I chirped to myself. 'Nothing to stop you now.'

Although I tried to fight it, the smallness of my room oppressed me right from the start. I stared at the walls as they crept closer to each other. My mind lapped at the windows, the ceiling, the door.

I wanted more. I wanted out.

I went for exploratory walks in the district, covering miles of dingy street, leaving the local patches of Green Belt to the joggers and flashers.

I soon stopped my daily trudge of the pavements. When I became too scared to go out. I was on the bus one day when a woman boarded. She was brutally fat, with a face full of wrath. She looked swollen with hatred. I couldn't breathe. I had to get off the bus and rush home. On my way through the streets I looked into the faces of every passerby. They stared back at me with stupid loathing.

Indoors again, I wept with relief. My room was a capsule, the one still point in the reeling universe. My safe sealed box.

I slept until afternoon most days, then dressed with supernatural slowness. I imagined my blood moving sluggish and muddy. Across the street a team of workmen were renovating a house. I watched them all winter chipping rubble, mixing cement, shouting, joking. I felt like David Attenborough observing a colony of miraculous scurrying insects. How I marvelled at their industry and purpose! Their energy incapacitated me even more. It was as if in some mysterious way my own strength were being siphoned off to complete the house. Soon I was dressing only on queuing day at the DHSS and Giro day when I went to the shops. I never saw my neighbours but I heard them. Above me someone watched television from breakfast-time right through to the white dot with no recuperation period. From next door lonelier noises. A woman and a man speaking in low urgent voices. Sporadic thumping of the bed. Sudden cries like the sounds that skydivers must make in the second before the parachute opens. The sort of cries that only God should have to listen to. Was it the same couple, I wondered, or a woman selling her body to a clutch of men? The act always took the same brief amount of time and followed the same pattern like some meticulously choreographed performance. The conversation was always rudimentary and unlaughing. This evidence could support either conclusion.

On bad days when I could feel the world spinning, the fucking seemed like a jibe at me. But most of my days were groggy and neutral.

Sometimes I was surprised to overhear myself thinking: 'You must get a job' or 'It's time you married again.' I knew I would never seek another job and the thought of marriage exhausted me. Honeymoons and champagne, routine ecstasies with lashings of spermicidal cream. Menus and budgets. I would have to jostle round supermarkets in a bright methodical way. I would have conversational obligations. Lying together every night. Lie-ing together. About ourselves, our pasts. I had done enough of that. Betraying my history into speech. Cosmetic tales. Or ugly plaintive little stories that were really saying: 'Love me love me/gimme gimme/save-my-soul/slave-my-soul. . .'

The room on the other side of mine was empty until Cornelius Lloyd moved in. Stormed in. Secretly I changed his name to Loud, and when I really knew him, I changed it to Lout. The first day he arrived there was a heartstopping sound like machine gun fire at my door. It was Lout banging the Shakespeare. He stepped expertly past me when I opened the door.

'Just come to introduce myself,' he announced. 'I like to establish contact right away.' My sofa was littered with paperback books, so he sprawled on the bed. A beefy black guy with big round eyes and cropped woolled hair. He was dressed in a track suit and training shoes which he planted considerately on my white bedspread. My voice was weak from lack of use.

'Would you like a cup of tea?' I whispered.

'Nothing stronger?' he asked.

I was treated to his whole biography that night. And most subsequent nights without variation of plot or language. He was attending a college of further education, although there was no point in studying. His English teacher hated him and always gave him low grades despite his warnings. He would fix him. He had ways. His Mathematics teacher fancied him something rotten. She was always touching him with her moist white paws. He might oblige her if he felt charitable enough. No one escaped his condemnation: parents, girlfriends, mates, relatives, strangers in the street. . . He was a sports addict and never tired of congratulating himself on his prowess at swimming, running, weight-training. It seemed to me that his mouth was the most exercised part of him. Sometimes he would fire his attention at me. 'Come on, give us a smile!' It reminded me of the compulsory joy I had to display in my infant Sunday school when Jesus wanted me for a sunbeam. He treated me with an abusive edgy courtliness, always haranguing me with dispiriting advice.

'You never have no fun. Why don't you get a guy? Your tits aren't bad.

Why don't you learn to type like the other chicks?

12

You could be a secretary, marry the guv'nor, if you play your cards right.

You should take some exercise, Fatso.'

One night I reached for my cigarettes, and he grabbed my wrist.

'Don't smoke. It's filthy.'

'Get your hands off me.'

'I don't want you polluting my air.'

'It's my air. It's my room. I don't want you in it.' He laughed, not believing me.

'Please leave. Now.'

He skulked towards the door. 'You're not very neighbourly.' When he was half out, he turned and said: 'You're on smack, am I right? I can get you some supreme stuff!'

'No.'

I thought he wouldn't bother me again, but he was back the next night, repossessing the bed. 'I've come to keep you company,' he announced, as if he had sacrificed some glamorous social occasion to attend to a welfare case. He went to my fridge and took a swig of milk from the bottle. Liquid was dribbling down his chin. I wanted to kill him. He started his usual litany of menaces and complaints about his hordes of enemies. I could see an erection through his clingy pants. I wanted rid of him, his unmanageable piece of gristle, his rippling ebony biceps, his spicy sausage smell. He had invaded my refuge. I decided to make my body the still point of the turning world. I would be safe inside the ghetto of my own flesh. At once I felt stronger. His words started to bounce off me and fall dead in heaps.

I hit on an idea. Switched on my tape recorder and inserted the microphone. Lout went on with his hatespew, not noticing, as I guessed he wouldn't.

'Hey, listen to this,' I said later. I played it loud and booming. It was Lout at his moronic best.

Whinge/rant/sulk/gripe/growl. I switched to the wrong speed, chasing his voice into a squeaky garble, back to normal speed again. He looked as if I'd caught him pissing his pants.

'You white cow,' he said, full of wonder and admiration. 'You filthy Irish white cow.'

I was kneeling to rewind the tape when suddenly Lout jerked me back on to the floor, my bent legs trapped beneath my pelvis. The pain in my thighs made my eyes stream. Lout held me by the throat and knees.

'I think you're going a bit bonkers cooped up in here. You need some exercise, stretch your back a bit.'

'Let me up. Please.'

He raised his fists. 'See, no hands.'

I could not raise my tilted trunk or release my legs. There was a wrenching pain in my lower back.

'Help me,' I begged, reaching my hands towards him.

'You soft snivelling girl.' He placed one hand right in my crotch, the other round my neck and levered me into an upright position. It was a deft surprising movement which filled me with guilt and glee. The tickling sensation between my legs remained. I pretended to massage my knees, then stood up slowly.

'It's getting late. Don't let me detain you.'

'Aw, for God's sake! Can't you take a joke? No wonder you got no friends. You're so damned unneighbourly.'

'I'm tired. I want to go to bed.'

'What's stopping you?'

'You.'

'I could crumple you like paper,' he said quietly. 'I could rip you apart.'

'You're so damned unneighbourly.'

He went and I wept in a way that gave me no relief. Short of murder, there seemed to be no way to get rid of him. I knew it was the utter vacancy of my life that legitimized his colonization of it. I was manless, jobless, pointless. If only my life could have a purpose, then I might be allowed to inhabit it on my own terms. I must find a vocation, some passion that would not involve excursions into the outside world. World. Whirled. Words. Words were what I loved and respected. 'Tower of Words.' Someone used to call me that. Listen to these: forlorn, lechery, scalp, lilt, catatonia, desolate, snow-drift, discourse. The magic of words, the way reality bends to them. When I was a child I used to whisper 'Goddeslove' to myself to banish my fear of the dark. I didn't know it was 'God-is-love' slurred together or what it meant. And when I was in school, I had only to say 'Dissociate' to myself and the imbecilic faces of my teachers would shrink and recede. Words have power, and power was what I lacked.

I decided to become a writer. That would be my excuse for living. And for banning Lout from my room. Next day I bought paper and pencils. But I couldn't write. I could only draw. My father's face with a jutting penis where the nose should be. My husband's beard composed

14

of worms. My mother in a party dress rucked up to her waist. Expelling a foetus from her anal passage. I started to draw Lout. Empty sockets where the eyes should be. Elongated swollen lips battening on to a deflated breast. Droplets of milk spattering his chin. Suddenly I laughed freely for the first time in months. He was nothing but a babymouth yearning for the nearest suckle!

I began to write. I was equal to it, although it was the hardest work I had ever done. In the solitude of my room, I summoned and dismissed presences at will. I overheard the thoughts of strangers. I unpoliced my memory, and it was as if I had died and could relive everything without pain. I knew I had found a way to rescue myself. I shoved a note under Lout's door to inform him that there would be no more dazzling soirées in my boudoir. I wasn't scared; he had shrunk to his correct size. But of course he did not want to pull his weight in my new conception of myself. For a few nights he whined at the door. 'I only want to say hello, for Christ's sake. God, some people! You try to be nice, where does it get you?'

I lay down until he went away. On Giro day I rushed round the shops, eager to get back home to my work. Lout was lounging on my bed when I entered.

'How did you get in here?'

'I have ways,' he grinned at me.

'You can't stay.'

He rose and cupped my face in his hands. 'You haven't washed your hair for ages, have you?' He sounded wistful.

'Oh no, I forgot! Been so busy. Is it disgusting?'

He pulled me gently down on the bed. 'If you had washed it, it would have spread out like a fan on the pillow. Like feathers.' His hand lingered on my hair for hardly a moment. I felt sorry for him, as if I had cheated him. He kissed me with a shocking sweetness. Pulled off his clothes and straddled me. Making his presence felt for once without opening his mouth.

He strips me and I wait breathless, expecting him at any moment to change into himself and denounce the pallor and softness of my skin. This doesn't happen. His body moves on me, a broad black blade. His face falls towards me and falls towards me, until I no longer need eyes to see him. His blackness is filling me and I am not afraid. I remember the childhood blackness of my bedroom, the blackness of nightmares, forest fires, coalmine disasters, cancer, death, sin, secrets. I am not afraid. I clasp him tight.

15

'You see,' he giggles, *'no one can resist me.'*

If this were a piece of fiction, I would end it there on that teasingly ambiguous, faintly lyrical note. Same with a film. It would end with the crucified grateful grin of a fucked woman, as is expected. Or I could be blasphemous and let the camera spy on the man's face. Yes, I would give you a vision of Lout at his manly exertions, his deep frown, his weighted lids, the charming flecks of spittle in the corners of his mouth. But this is real life. Reader, I didn't marry him. He disappeared into the building like the other tenants, moved out some time without saying goodbye. I didn't decide to keep the baby. I just kept it. I did not think of it as a cellular blob. It was an eye, a wakeful eye floating in my womb. I know I could have gone to doctors, I could have stuck my feet in their stirrups, opened my legs to their killing machine. But I didn't. Maybe it's because I've had enough of death one way or another. Maybe it's because I'm a fool, a victim, a slob. I stopped writing my book, took up my old sleepful life which was just waiting to reclaim me. Sometimes I used to play the tape of Lout's diatribe, which must be a clue to the dangers of living in a low-stimulus environment.

One morning when I was gazing out of the window, I noticed a slogan on one of the workmen's shirts: NUKE THE ARGIES.

'Nuke'? 'Argies'? Argentinians?

What was Argentina to do with anything? I couldn't believe or understand what I was seeing. It could not be 'nuke'; it must read 'I like' or something. My eyesight was faulty. That was it: I had morbid eyesight! Later I retrieved an unsullied Sunday newspaper from one of the bins outside and read about the Task Force 'mission' to the Falklands. Saw the festive pictures of the fleet's send-off from Portsmouth. Women waving handkerchiefs and Union Jacks. Embracing their men or just watching, their faces glowing with pride and excitement. On the huge ship, a banner: SOCK IT TO 'EM, BOYS! I couldn't believe it. Britain was heading to war. Brittania. Troops setting sail to reclaim John Bull's Other Other Island. Sock It To 'Em. Nuke the Argies. Murder is Big Fun.

Don't think about it, I told myself. This is not your country. But I could not banish it from my mind. Memories of my life in Belfast surged back, images of that same bloodlust. A woman dancing with glee and screaming at an injured Civil Rights marcher: 'Fenian blood! I want to see Fenian blood!' My own father crowing over the televised deaths of marchers on Bloody Sunday: 'Slap it into them! They had it coming!'

16

Those blunt aggressive words with their comic-strip notion of death: sock, slap, nuke.

I went to bed, shivering like a dog in a storm. Nothing was inviolate. No room, no womb, no indifference.

Jane Eyre

2

New Parents

My abdomen began to balloon and swell. The breasts were heavy and unbearable to touch. The teeth ached. Night and day I craved food.

I had no plan for the future; I had no plan for the present.

To get food, I had to make daily excursions. Past the gents' toilet at the end of the street with its jangling red graffiti:

'Men stink.'

'May we burn alive.'

Past the dark taxicab office window, where my reflection always surprised me. I expected to see shadows beneath the eyes, savage indentations round the mouth. But my face was smooth, innocent and bright!

I was broke but I used only the best shops. My roomy pockets were able to hold many small luxury items; crab, salmon, cream, gift wrapped chocolates, fudge, pâté, dates. I filled the legitimate basket with cheaper fare: beans, potatoes. My throat was so tight I could only mutter to the cashier. I tried to avoid the necessity for speech. Although I grew accomplished at my task, taking and taking without being taken, I remained frightened. I had never known before such a voluptuous panic. But I loved my smug homecomings! Spreading my plunder on the floor, gloating.

I grew bolder, started stocking up on things for the baby: a pram quilt, a packet of bibs decorated with cute cartoon animals, romper suits in snowy white and primrose yellow. I scorned those coy strictures: 'blue for a boy, pink for a girl.' Pink. Pretty insipid pink. The colour of femininity, homosexuality, inferiority, exclusion. I would not dress my child in pink any more than I would dress her in swaddling clothes. 'But she's black, black,' a mean, mocking voice in my head would chant at me.

I remembered Cornelius at those moments. His complaints, his daily humiliations. He seemed to be always running the gauntlet between two white walls, prodded by vicious stares, sly whisperings of 'nigger' and 'black bastard'.

I ate like a pig, eyeless and insatiable. The cool sanity of green apples, the placid warmth of beans, salty smoothness of melted cheese, crunchy sweetness of chocolate bars. I could go on. I will go on. After all, didn't I risk everything to get those feasts? I filled my room and nostrils with cooking smells, nothing else quickened my heartbeat, nothing else made me tap my foot with impatience. So: the tart taste of thin yoghurt, white chewiness of chicken breasts. Heavenly addictive fried potatoes. Bananas with those telltale brown spots indicating their ripeness for guzzling. I was living from hand to mouth. The food made my life bearable, a picnic basket in the vale of tears.

Of course there was disgust and nausea after these arduous dinners. I became eaten in my turn, consumed with guilt, gnawed by remorse. Lay stunned on my bed, picturing my fat-encrusted heart, my blood thick with cholesterol. I wondered if the baby was able to snatch any goodness from the sea of muck bubbling in my entrails; some vitamins and minerals, jewels among the junk. And sometimes I could imagine her. A wistful embryonic face floating in the safe darkness. She was growing steadily, a clever accretion cell by cell, unstoppable. Behind her face, the barest hint of a soul. There must be a soul, because I was dreaming her dreams, quiet drifting dreams, not mine at all. There must be a soul. An irreplaceable unique soul? Immortal. . .? Is there?

I cut down my shopping trips. I could feel my luck running thin, my guilt hanging out of me like the springs protruding from my old mattress. My shoulder started to flinch in anticipation of the lawful hand. I sat for hours in the botanic gardens, like someone mugged by life, surrounded by tall overblown tulips that looked like stately pink goblets. Then I would walk back home through the sunny streets where my bulging shadow resembled a fat old woman. Men looked at me with resentment when they bothered to look at all. Once I heard a story about a stripper, I hope it's true. She was performing in a men's club. *She dances and undulates with her back to the audience, removing the skimpy garments in that playful complicated way, glancing over her shoulder to throw out those practised slave-smiles full of dangerous hospitality. 'Turn round, turn round,' the men clamour. They grow desperate, they beg, insult, threaten. 'Turn round, give us a peep, darlin', let us see yah, slag, bitch, whore. . .'*

Watch her start to turn, as she must, as she surely must, for it is expected, and hasn't she been paid? Doesn't she understand? Yes, majestically, slowly, she turns and turning shows a face that's proud and free, treacherous tits perched on top of a perfect globe, her massive pregnant belly. Groans of fury and distress from the betrayed punters. Sounds of retching and puking and the swinging exit door.

Women smiled at me. Benevolent conspiratorial covetous smiles. My body was no longer an aimless assemblage of busy gurgling pipes. It was purposeful flesh, tenanted and privileged. 'Mother.' I blossomed in the shade of that word, receiving the smiles and nods from strangers like little sprinklings of holy water.

'You're first,' a voice spoke to me one day in the park. I looked round startled to see a woman seating herself on the bench beside me.

'Yes, I was here first,' I said snappishly, not wanting any contact with any human being whatsoever. She laughed delightedly: 'I mean, is it your first?'

'Oh, yes, it is.'

'I've just had a baby. He's three months old. Do you know what sex?'

'She's a girl.'

'Where did you get your amniocentesis?'

'Amnio-? I haven't. I just know it's a girl.'

'Oh. Would you be very disappointed if it turned out to be a boy?'

'It's not a boy.'

'A lot of people prefer girls. To dress up. Let their hair grow long. Some people say girls are more docile.'

'I don't want to dress her up! I don't want a plaything.'

She grinned, 'Just testing you. Know what I hate? Little girls with pierced ears!'

'Oh so do I! What was the birth like? I mean, did it hurt?'

'Yes. No! I can't recall. When is your baby due?'

'The fifth of November.'

'You must be in the same hospital as I was. St Mary's?'

'I haven't finalised my arrangements yet.'

'But you should! Your doctor must be a fool.'

I confessed suddenly. That I had no doctor. No husband. No money. I thought she would be repelled, tell me I had no sense, no morals, no business having a child. But no! She was full of ideas and advice, giving me the name of a good doctor, a single parent organisation. She knew all about social security allowances, jumble sales, natural childbirth classes. She urged me to attend a class but I said I didn't want to lie on a

20

floor practising community panting. I made her laugh by describing the various exercise classes I had attended in the past. The yoga sessions which began and ended with obligatory amorous obeisances to some crosslegged geriatric guru and were interspersed with much chanting of 'Om'. The keep-fit classes led by an emaciated stick-insect with the yell of a martinet: 'Work those buttocks! Come on, I wanta see some sweat! Squeeze! Kick! Lift! Higher, I mean higher!'

But despite my reluctances, I was growing excited. My new friend was called Caroline. She made me see childbirth as something you could *succeed* at. I longed to be as chic, enterprising and clued up about it as she was.

'Let's go and have a coffee,' she said impulsively. I hesitated and she touched my arm in a way that was not spontaneous. 'Yes, that's what we'll do. You need cheering up, don't you?'

In the café, Caroline told me she was an actress. 'Oh, not famous, of course. I don't expect I shall ever be famous.' I realized that secretly she yearned for fame. I began to be uneasy about her loud, merry laugh, her attentive way of tilting her head as she listened to me, the way she soaked up glances from people around us. Was she on automatic pilot, practising her craft?

'What about the guy? The Father?' she pronounced it with mock piety.

'Gone.'

'Gone but not forgotten?'

'Left a reminder, didn't he? You're married, I see.'

'Yes, for my sins.'

'Is he glad about your baby?'

'Bloody ecstatic! Oh, he's very good, really. I'm a pampered woman. As he is always keen to point out. . . Why don't you come round and see us? Have a look at the baby? He's lovely! Tomorrow?'

I agreed. I wanted to see her again. On my way home, I joined the local library and loaded myself with ante-natal care books and some works on the Brontës.

Back home I scrubbed and cleansed my ignoble room, the corridor, and the bathroom, making the toilet bowl, sink, and bath lilywhite and gleaming apart from ineradicable deposits of limescale. My child must not cohabit with dirt. Something was happening. To do with my talking to Caroline. It made the baby real. I resolved that next day I would visit the doctor and get myself booked into a hospital. Suddenly my for-real baby fluttered and I screamed. The fog which I inhabited cleared, leaving me blinking and helpless. What the hell had I been dreaming of? That I could just stay in my room, and one fine day the baby would slide out of me, I would bite through the bloody cord, make a cup of tea and carry on as normal? I needed knowledge, assistance, hands to hold me in the spasms of birth, hands to coax her out of me. But O God, what would happen? What would they do when they discovered that I was harbouring a black fatherless child? How their lips would curl at my single room, my penniless state! Maybe I should give my girl away to some deserving couple full of money and certainties? I started to cry, assailed by an image of myself lying beneath Cornelius in that posture of defeat, being ridden like an animal. My child was a mistake, the pitiless result of a crazy sexual act which should have dissolved into forgetfulness like some tawdry dream. The world had sneaked into me in an unguarded moment and now I would never be alone again, could not afford to be alone. I could not bear the awful vulnerability of the body, its gateless holes that would only be plugged in death. Yes, great swabs of gauze stuffed into the lifeless body to prevent emission of gases! Death, the biggest joke. Why should I endure this agonizing slowness of gestation? Why must I have a child who would draw every drop of love out of me, a child destined for death and putrefaction? Women give life, they say, but we're really feeding death, labouring for death. 'Cunt', I thought of that sullen word that men use to mean the woman herself, not just the hunted hated rip in her flesh. And it's not only the sleazos and the creeps who think like that, but the intellectual 'giants' like Sartre. 'Woman is a slimy gaping hole. She represents nothingness.'

I was a fermenting bog, a piece of perforated flesh that could be penetrated by the penis, the finger, the broken bottle, invaded by germs and sperms.

I begged my baby to die, to release herself and drain away.

Get out! Get out!

I went into the corridor that was filled with a new neighbour's junk: ski boots, old shelves, a broken telephone, a bike. The bike. I started to wheel it. A loud whirring of spokes. I stopped. Listened. My breathing the only sound. 'Nobody's home,' I thought. 'I am nobody's home.'

Out on to the landing. A big effort to haul the machine downstairs.

Out on to the street.

Out! Out! Out!

I rode the way I remembered from before, heading away from the heavy traffic, the breezes whipping my face. Suddenly, a cobbled road, a godsend! I laughed out loud as my limbs juddered.

That'll rock you, baby! That'll knock you off your pedestal!

Yes, my womb was a sliding chute, yes, a greasy pole. . . Let me go, please let me go. . . Sweat was stinging my eyes. I had to slow down, but rode on steadily, mile after mile.

Past children playing. Unnecessary children playing unnecessary games.

Past menacing youths, shaven-headed and tattooed. Not guilty, not guilty, I told them.

Finito, c'est fini, fini.

O Death, where is thy sting?

A car horn hooted. 'Fucking cyclist!'

Better go home, I decided. Before the blood comes.

'I've done my best for you, baby. Never say I didn't try to protect you.' *death*

She didn't die. I didn't die. If you have tears, prepare to weep elsewhere.

I took myself to the doctor's where I was palpated, probed, measured, weighed, interrogated, and scolded for my belated concern.

I attended natural childbirth classes, where I had to look nonchalant during advice on how to decide if my husband should be present at the birth, when to resume lovemaking, and how to ensure that he wouldn't be made jealous of the 'new arrival'. Caroline and I went to films once a week in the afternoon, and sometimes I visited her home, which was comfortable and cluttered with interesting things or with things that were meant to be interesting. When she was alone with me, Caroline was sharp and animated, but when her husband was present, she became langourous. He called her Caro. He was older than her, blonde and glossy, dressed with a carelessness that might have been unplanned. A Professor of English Literature, always leavening his conversation with bits of remembered poetry, suitable or unsuitable to the moment.

The couple played a tireless teasing game with each other: sulks, truces, caresses and thumps. Sometimes Dominic would flirt with me, calling me Mariana, reading a poem 'especially for you', offering sweets or wine ceremoniously. Caroline would taunt him then with questions in mock-aggrieved tones: 'Wouldn't you like to offer Fran more coffee? Don't you want to show her the garden? It's so full of flowers and nature. . . Would you two like to talk undisturbed?'

In the presence of a witness, they shone more brightly to each other. I knew they were using me to top up their level of arousal, but I didn't care. I loved being there, sinking into their velvet sofa, stroking their grey cat, escaping to their cool green bathroom, where I gazed into their vast mirror. And saw a woman transfixed and dreaming, without happiness but without dread. On Caroline's birthday in August we had a celebration, just the three of us. We ate steak and chips with salad, chocolate mousse, drank champagne and special expensive coffee.

At the end of the meal, Caroline stood up, tipsy and glaring, raising her glass in a toast: 'To Dominic, who paid for it all!' she said so spitefully that we froze. She laughed, releasing us.

At home I was reading a lot, stuffing brain now as well as stomach. Biographies of the Brontës and their works: *Villette*, *Wuthering Heights*, *Jane Eyre*, Emily's poetry. Emily fascinated me, and I found myself sometimes whispering lines from her work and it felt like praying: 'And hide me from the hostile light.' 'No coward soul is mine.'

Those words made me strong and excited. But why did Emily die so early? Why did she brave death instead of life? This woman who loved the earth, who once painted heaven as a place of exile, Catherine crying to Nelly: 'Heaven did not seem to be my home, and I broke my heart with weeping to come back to earth.'

I read over and over the account of her last two months of life, Charlotte's despairing letters. Emily refused to see a doctor, would not rest, rejected all remedies, advice, sympathy. She did not explain herself, would scarcely allow any allusion to her illness. Her family had to watch in restrained anguish as Emily, emaciated and breathless, went about her daily tasks. On her final day she rose and dressed, the rattle of death sounding in her throat. This was no resigned sinking into death, it was a resolute summoning, an *earning* of death. Is this true? Was she angry? Did she really will herself to die? Was it grief over Branwell's bitter unhappiness and death? The menace of Anne's tuberculosis, pronounced incurable? The uncomprehending malice of her reviewers? Loss of faith? Of inspiration?

Any of these? All of these? None?

It cannot be known. It cannot be found out. She is like the prisoner in one of her own poems, confined behind triple walls. Unreachable behind the barricades of her silence, her strangeness, her strength. When I thought of her stoic unwhimpering death, I was awestruck, miserable, and always finally exasperated. Oh, what was she but a

24

sex-starved religioso, half in love with death like all the Irish? But I worshipped her.

My child, my little black Celt, would be called Emily. With that name I wanted to confer on her power and truthfulness, the strength to follow beauty. I hoped she would share Emily's love of the earth and not my vision of the world in which the dungheap and the skulls loomed large. No, let her wear her blackness all outside of herself! Let her look at the world with the same equanimity as God must, with equal tenderness for shit and gold, belching and music. Or equal indifference.

Caroline had hated pregnancy but I enjoyed the changing sensations of my body. In the early months there were the almost impalpable ripples, sometimes the ghost of a touch, that made me visualize the shift of my baby's transparent finger or her misshapen skull. She was a lazy fish in her warm water. Later there were more vigorous movements that jolted my own frame. I could never have imagined before this unbroken intimacy of two bodies, this endless unity. It made me wonder if the hunger for sex is a kind of nostalgia. . .

'What do you think of "Emily"?' I asked.
   'Old-fashioned.'
   'Yes,' I agreed happily.
   Caroline sighed: 'Is this final, or can you be talked out of it?'
   'Final.'
   'OK. Let's celebrate.'
   'Let's celebrate,' was Caroline's slogan. She had a talent and a desire for snatching moments from the daily conveyor belt. She liked to dress them up into something festive. We had routine outings and treats, which we always 'deserved'. Besides, they were a way of 'killing time'. I hated it when Caroline said that. I always remembered that time was killing us, but such observations were unwelcome to her, so I kept quiet. Caroline paid for our outings, which worried me at first. When I used to earn money, I never would let men buy me anything, even a drink. I didn't want to work off debts in bed. And now I was helping Caroline to spend Dominic's money. Did I imagine that his uxorious possessive smile sometimes now included me? Why was I often reluctant to disagree with his opinions?

They don't care about money, I told myself. Why should you?

Caroline needed a partner in indulgence. She hated to go out alone. She felt less spoilt if she was exercising charity at the same time. I was her necessary companion, her absolution, her good deed.

She was always fretting about the 'loss' of her figure, and exercising manically to get it back. She took to parading herself spitefully before the mirror; 'inspecting the ruin' she called it. One morning she ordered a taxi and took us off to a forbidding Mayfair salon for a 'Top to Toe'. In the foyer we read the schedule of this massive overhaul which was to last all day and include a lunch break (low calorie, vitamin-packed) and 'grooming education' from Mr Cedric. Draped in kimonos, we struggled upstairs. Caroline was whisked off at once. It was lovely to watch her, an idle queen surrounded by attendants, one kneeling to file her toenails, one plucking her eyebrows, one standing by respectfully, waiting to do her hair. I was led to my 'consultation'. My advisor was a young Cockney called André. He lifted clumps of my hair with distaste as if it were some kind of striated dung.

'It's the fantasy element that's missing,' he announced. 'Look at it! No shape. No colour. I'm surprised you can be bothered to have hair at all!' His own locks were long and lank, oily with gel or natural grease. I resisted his persuasion, rejected his album of spiky feather multicoloured tresses. His face was that of a spurned missionary. 'Oh well, if you're not interested in your beauty potential, some people just aren't into transformation.'

During the shampoo he scrubbed my scalp viciously.

During the cutting, he tugged and pulled. 'Abuse comes expensive,' I thought. But I enjoyed the rest of the 'treatments' and massages.

Back home, Caroline and I stared at our perfected selves. Suddenly, she said: 'You've never seen the whole of our house, have you?' I didn't confess that I had peeped in every room on my first excursions to the bathroom.

'Come on,' she said. 'The grand tour.'

She lingered in the spare room. 'Peaceful, isn't it? And quite large, really.'

A few days later, the proposition.

'Fran,' she said experimentally. 'How about coming to live here?'

'What?'

'Close your mouth, dear. Just think of the mutual advantages. How can you stay in that slum?'

'Easy. All it requires is no money.'

'You can't inflict it. . . . Listen, I want to work again, attend auditions. In this game, you've got to keep a high profile, stay to the fore in people's minds. It would be a great help if I knew you were here. I'd be free to work and seek work without hassle. And when I'm at home, we'd be company; cut down the tedium of the nappies and squalls, wouldn't it?'

'I don't know. I have to think.'

'About what?'

'What if it doesn't work out? Emily and I would be the cuckoo and the cuckoo's mother.'

'But we've never had a cross word.'

'I've never been your employee. And what about Dominic?'

'Dominic is in favour.'

'You've discussed it? What did he say?'

'Oh, Dominic wants what I want. Two hearts that beat as one, you know?'

'Is he in his study? I think I'll go and see him, if you don't mind.'

'You don't have to ask my permission.'

There was no reply when I tapped at his door. I opened it slightly and saw him hunched over a spread of papers and books on his desk.

'Am I disturbing you?'

'No. I've reached an impasse.'

'What are you writing?'

'A lecture on Eliot.'

'George or T.S.?'

'Which do you prefer?

'You can't compare them.'

He laughed. 'No, of course. But it is my job to compare the incomparable. For the benefit of the uncomprehending.'

'Dominic? How do you feel about the prospect . . . the possibility of me moving here. To take care. . .'

'I hope you will. I think it's a delightful and sensible solution to all our problems.'

'Won't you feel invaded? Two sets of nappies, two babies screaming in unison and separately. . .'

'I'd rather have a choir of babies screaming at me than Caro! Please do come. Consider it carefully.'

I rose to leave, suddenly shy as if I had been at an interview with a bank manager. But I stopped at his book-lined shelves.

'Dominic, do books help you to live?'

'Well,' he laughed in a kind of annoyance. 'I earn my living by them.'

27

'But you know what I mean.'

'Yes. They help me to live. To live second-hand. Sometimes I feel like a shopboy. A parasite.'

I was quiet.

'You're supposed to contradict me! Tell me what a deathblow to Culture it would be if I stopped teaching.'

'I hate it when people deny and minimize *my* feelings. "Oh don't exaggerate . . . it's not the end of the world . . . life is full of compromise and sacrifice. . ." Isn't there anything you like about your job?'

'Yes.'

'Well?'

'Giving lectures. *Delivering* lectures. Standing up there in front of all those bored remorseless faces that get younger every year. Knowing exactly what to say, every phrase apt and elegant, every joke intentional. So different from real life, you know. All those shifty silences, not saying what you mean, regretting it when you do.'

'I'm glad when I say what I mean. Even when it's terrible. It's like naming a disease. You feel more in control even if it's killing you.'

'What is killing you, Fran?'

He was staring at me and I couldn't move.

You don't have to get in bed with any man ever, I thought, not in any bed at all.

'It's not contagious,' I laughed, turning to inspect some books.

'You can borrow anything you like,' he offered. 'The modern novels are over here, behind me.'

'I'll come back and browse when you're not here, I mean, when you're not busy. Thanks.'

'Let us know soon what you decide,' he said as I made for the door. 'Because if you don't join us, I'll have to start looking around for an "au pair".' Maximum dejection in his voice.

I was glad to get out of his room. I had never noticed before his tight dissatisfied mouth. It made me remember my ex-husband, the innumerable ruined nights spent listening to his grievances.

'Your mouth has nothing to do with me,' I told Dominic silently.

'All settled, then?' Caroline asked. 'You took long enough.'

'No. I need time.'

'Suit yourself! But I don't see what the big problem is. You're such a bloody pessimist! No wonder you get on so well with Dominic.' She sounded pleased, accusing, and curious all at once.

28

'He seems a bit fed up with his job,' I volunteered.

'Oh nonsense! He loves it! Never out of his hideyhole when he's here, is he? Always working or pretending to work. And he dotes on his bloody students. Of course, it's the premenstrual poetesses he loves the best.'

'If I come here, I'll not be the umpire, you know.'

'Oh don't worry. I'm sure you'll be perfectly neuter.'

'Neuter! Is that what you think? That I'm some kind of frumpy non-person?'

'I said "neutral". N-E-U-T-R-A-L. Don't fly off the handle!'

When I went back to my room, it looked meaner and smaller than before. I was amazed at my own intrepid poverty. The thought of bringing the child there reduced me to tears. Would it even be permitted? I recalled all the sounds I had ever heard in that place. Earsplitting music played at all hours, unrestrained marital howlings and complaints. But never a dog's bark or a baby's cry. No children or pets, it was obvious. Yes! I began to feel light and happy. How great it would be to have no choice! I should jump at Caroline's offer. But I was scared. I would still be essentially homeless. A lodger. A kind of nanny. What an elderly demeaning word! The name of a goat. I was never at ease with Caroline and Dominic. Would I be at their mercy? At their beck and call? Would I have no breathing space? Maybe I would get snarled up in their squabbles. I was afraid not to be lonely. I was the sort of person who will not ask the way in the street, the sort of person who makes a phone call hoping that no one will answer. How could I think of. . .? But how could I not think of it? So, there were snags. But also temptations. The comfort and safety of their home. Their companionship. Two babies. To have and to hold. Two for the price of one, I enticed myself. Maternal greed was growing in me, strong and heedless.

3

Flesh

Caroline

She thought about herself continuously even though she was no one. Her body was the only real fact about her. She wanted to have orgasms. Men weren't necessary to that process, but there were always men. Caroline stared at them. She liked watching males, how they became themselves as they unpeeled their uniform suits and underwear that was either greying or gaudy. Each man was unique. She recalled some of them as vague entities, others in a dismembered way. A fleece of yellow hair, a strange mouth with one sensuous and one austere lip, *his* fine arms, that one's fingerthin penis, another's tangy scent.

Often there were surprises. A man with (or inside?) a pale intelligent body which seemed to be *listening* but turned wooden and ungiving in bed. Another time there was that hefty perspiring man who undressed himself under neon brightness like a drunk in the dark. She had watched with growing resignation, thinking that at least it would all be over in a couple of minutes. But he had touched and parted her flesh with thrilling reverential delicacy.

You couldn't always tell from their bodies how they would make love. Nor from their clothes and talk. Although there were certain features of dress and style, certain insignia, which automatically put men on Caroline's boycott list. She despised toupees, false teeth (that deadly white evenness!), curlicued Mexican moustaches, open-chested shirts revealing medallions nesting in swatches of hair, bulbous rings, digital watches, ritzy ties, nylon shirts, suede shoes, fake suntans, indiscreet aftershave. . .

Men who jumped the sartorial hurdles often failed the next ordeal. Bottom of the heap came (alas too swiftly) the premature ejaculators. Then the unfortunates ('never had any trouble before can't understand it') who couldn't get/keep it up. The more mannerly ones found or simulated a compensatory fervour in their fingers or tongues. Next the stuntmen with their tricksy routines; the woman-haters who skirted (deskirted?) their prey before conquering her. They sought to annihilate her charm by snatching it. The torrential talkers who got through reams of autobiography, exterior monologue, and eulogies of their wives: their ecstasies were all verbal. But sometimes, just sometimes there was a man who. . . Sometimes she sailed into a white silence. He helped her. An assisted passage.

She scrutinised these men, their eyes, the flecked irises, every thread of blood, the black gaps of their pupils. And then she forgot them. Faces fell away. Names fell away.

They were no one like her. Solid phantoms. Searching like her for a shortlived release from a makeshift identity.

'The pursuit of happiness': an accurate phrase, she always thought, as happiness seemed to be forever in full flight. Caroline's enemy was Time, the great stealer. It was Time that diluted, banalised everything. She remembered Alasdair's birth: The Birth, as Dominic called it. He was present, of course, the progenitor, unsqueamish modern husband equipped with natural sponge for mopping the maternal brow. She recalled everything in hallucinatory detail. The hurting lights overhead, the doctor's open pores, the agony that was like being disembowelled. In the middle of a white hot pain, she found herself looking straight at Dominic, his noble composed features. Deus ex machina. Her rectum emptied. Hate flowed from her mouth. Was she really saying all those things? She was being lowered into her grave, solicitous doggy faces peering down at her. If only spit could fly upwards!

'No epidural, no episiotomy', she had insisted when she was still a human being, in possession of imaginary rights. Out of mercy, caution, and disrespect, they gave her both.

'Just a little injection into the spine, it won't make you too drowsy, there's a good girl. . . Just the tiniest incision, can't have you tearing, can we?'

'It's a boy! You have a boy!' The air turned festive, all sins were forgiven.

They placed him, cleansed and crying, on to her abdomen. She saw him. Tears spilled down her face, her nipples engorged. He was astonishing. Thick black hair, tracery of blue veins at the temples, tight fists with perfect shell nails, the tiny sex soft and wrinkled. He looked tender and knowledgeable, a traveller from another more tranquil zone.

This must be love, she thought.

Dominic stayed with her for a couple of hours (special dispensation of the nursing staff). He was fulsome and happy, said he was 'humbled', 'grateful', 'transfigured'. In his euphoria, he restricted himself to one tasteless pun: Alasdair came 'trailing clouds of gory'.

He went home. Still Caroline could not rest. The world outside the window looked fresh and inviting. She had never tasted such good tea before! She was married to a rare and wonderful man. She had a perfect baby. She was pretty fabulous herself. Her life was beginning. Nothing could ever be drab and pointless again!

But of course. . . Of course. Time ran its of course. Soon she was resentfully glad to leave Alasdair with babysitters. Sometimes she even went out *nowhere* just to experience that lightness in her body that rose when she refused all that neediness, his need of her, her need of his need.

And Dominic . . . their rekindled love soon guttered. In fact, his physical coldness, his apparent *distaste* for her, increased, making her regret his witnessing of the birth. She suspected that he must see her now as some kind of disgusting larva. Although sometimes he looked at her with a kind of desire, but it was a desire so poignant and ethereal, as if he were beyond sex.

Those miraculous moments were only a flash in the pan, she thought. Like rainbows and shooting stars. You couldn't capture or congeal them. You couldn't repeat them or communicate them. How long before Lazarus yawned and scratched himself?

Her first meeting with Dominic had been full of that deceptive magic. He came along at a time when she was growing dissatisfied with her work. The distance between her passionate roles and her puny self was too depressing. She felt like the dimmest pilot light to be ignited only by borrowed emotion. She stopped calling her agent, gave auditions a miss.

But she hated her own company. Lovers were everywhere that Spring, arms laced, turning to gaze at each other like flowers drinking sunlight.

Why could it not be. . .? Why was she left out? Need for love spread through her like spite. Often she had to comfort friends recuperating from broken affairs. She envied them. At least they felt something, even if they only felt used! For Caroline, pain was it own absence.

One day she was dining with her friend Alex, another 'resting' actor, in a pizzeria near Covent Garden.

'I'll have the Seafood Special,' he ordered.

'I want profiteroles and extra cream,' she decided.

'Why can't you eat a main course like a decent person?'

'Don't like pizza.'

'Well, you might have said! We could have gone somewhere. . .'

'It doesn't matter.'

'How do you keep your skin so delectable? Choccies appear to be your staple diet!'

She shrugged. 'Just lucky.'

He stroked his own cheek nervously. 'When I'm thirty, I'll look like a raddled gnome.'

'Who says?' she guessed at once that the prediction was the parting gift of some disgruntled lover.

'Anyway, I'll be so charismatic by then, it won't matter.'

Caroline studied him. He was wearing a turquoise jump-suit. A recent permanent wave had turned his hair into a flossy protuberance that dwarfed his face. Everything about him advertised a bedroom pet. Except his eyes, which were serious and haunted and made him look like a distressed imp.

'Maybe you'll meet Mr Nutkins,' she soothed. It was his nickname for Mr Right.

'How's *your* love life?' he said cruelly.

'No one special.'

'No candidates for your crotch, you do surprise me!'

She became aware that a lone diner at the next table was listening to them attentively. With Alex, the more intimate the dialogue, the louder the volume.

'You're very wise. Men are absolute shits,' Alex said.

Caroline glanced at the eavesdropper. He smiled at her, a complicated adult smile. And she smiled back. Declaring . . .what? Independence? Betrayal of Alex? Sexual hope?

'. . .And most of them are useless in bed!' Alex went into a frenzied pantomime of gasping and jiggling followed by a swift collapse into snores.

'Gosh, Alex, has something extra-bad happened?'

But she wasn't listening to him any more. The other man was staring openly at her. His look was strange, not inquisitive, but both merciful and fiery, a look that said: 'I know' and 'Don't worry' and 'Something is about to happen.' She returned his gaze. Alex observed them and rose huffily. 'I've got to fly, Caroline. You won't mind if I leave this billette with you?'

'I'm Dominic Dalziel,' the man said as soon as Alex had departed. Exchange of data. Display of bare ring fingers. The old mating dance.

'And your wife, is she an academic also?' — 'Oh, I'm not married.' ('Take me, I'm yours.') . . .'And I was so lucky to find a good house. Too big for one, really!'

Suddenly Dominic leaned over and dabbed at the corner of her mouth. 'Chocolate,' he grinned.

It was such an ambivalent gesture, a bold declaration of intent, and yet so harmless, impersonal, like adjusting a crooked picture in passing.

Caroline was totally disarmed. She knew that this man was going to touch her everywhere.

They went back to his house. For coffee. Ground. French, several cups of.

Puzzlement. Caroline felt like an elated skier careering down a slope, miraculously halted and turned to ice. Her conversation was stilted: she was not prepared for conversation. Dominic drove her home. Mild fraternal kiss. What had she done wrong? She consulted the mirror, which yielded no answer. Perhaps older men adhered to a different sexual etiquette? He was thirty-three, after all. All weekend she stayed in, hanging round the phone, mute black instrument of torture. She read the papers from cover to cover. Two youths had committed a homosexual act in Hyde Park, egged on by cheering spectators. Improvised street theatre. And she could not even accomplish her modest and blameless desire behind closed curtains!

Dominic rang a few days later. She was cool, almost reluctant to see him again. But they did meet as they must, for was it not written in the stars, on the sands, on the lavatory walls?

During their long courtship, Dominic kept a gracious distance. Her whole body grew alert to his touch, his guiding hand on her elbow or her spine as he, the good shepherd, steered her across roads and through crowds. Dominic had the mystery of an orphan or an amnesiac. His allusions to his childhood were bitter but cryptic. He never saw his relatives. He was equally secretive about ex-lovers. They stayed wrapped in their shrouds. Caroline was glad. There was no one she must outdazzle or pay for. She decided that this relationship must be consummated and bought a new dress to step out of at the crucial moment. She confessed her virginity to Dominic like a shameful disease.

'Defloration,' he said with a shudder. 'To deflower. I'll be first, then. You'll never forget me.'

'Of course I'll forgive you!'

'That's not what I said.'

It was passionless that first time, almost tokenistic, the staking of a claim. Nothing was transformed except her future.

Some 'future'! Perhaps it was simply the past recycled in disguise? For she was as alone now as she had been in her father's house. It made her wince to remember her self-congratulations on finding a husband so utterly different from her father. And outwardly, Dominic did seem to possess every quality her father lacked: wit, culture, idealism.

But he doled out the same emotional pittance. Dominic, the bloodless blonde. *Blood*. That was the smell of Caroline's childhood. Her father was a butcher by trade, a thin rigorous man with pale indoors skin and purple lips. He brought home the bacon all right. And all other varieties of flesh and fowl, tough and tender. Caroline visited his shop once. . . Was she eight? Nine? She wandered round the back to the cold stores, where the assistants worked. It was like a crude operating theatre with its snowy slabs and cutting instruments, and that same faint stench of blood and fat, which was her father's aura. Three carcasses were suspended from hooks.

'What are they?' she asked Frankie, the only person who acknowledged her.

'Bullocks.'

'What's bullocks?'

'Know what a bull is? Sort of like a bull with a part missing. Only dead now. They're dead bullocks, so they're not bullocks no more.'

'Where's their heads?'

'Decapitated. Cut off.' He made a slashing gesture with his blade. 'Sold separate, they are, the heads. They scrape the flesh off the bones, eyes and all, shove the lot through the mincer and there's your mincemeat.'

'That's a lie!'

'God's truth, or I'm a vegetarian!'

'What's a vegetarian?'

'Know a lot, don't you? A vegetarian is someone who wants to put me out of a job.'

She had a vision of bullocks' heads lined up on a table, eyes open and filled with the glaze of death. Frankie began to carve a mound of meat, whistling and smiling at her from time to time. He looked exactly right for a butcher with his mottled salami cheeks and beefy arms.

'Was it you that made them dead?' she asked suddenly, indicating the carcasses behind him. They had stopped looking like hunks of inert matter and she was afraid.

'Me? No, do me a favour!'

He described the techniques of the abattoir, the stunning, the slitting of throats and bellies, the blood that brimmed in the runnels. How they removed the skin and the red squeaking entrails. . . Her hands were over her ears now, but she knew what he was saying. After that she could not load her fork at meal times without the sensation of spearing a living creature. She liked to watch her father, his eyes hard and black like a swan's, when he grumbled 'I'm not made of money, you know!' She thought, always with a thrill of disgust: 'Blood money.' His business was flourishing, but he hated to part with cash. Money was not there to be spent, but to be hoarded, increased, invoked.

The family meals were frugal, always unsold meat on the brink of going 'off', beans and greens. Holidays and treats had to be a bribe or some kind of investment: 'Promise Daddy you'll get good marks in school if. . .' And those awful Christmases, when he wore a paper crown on his sober mercantile head! She had to petition him for new shoes, clothes, school outings. He would think about her requests, and the longer he pondered, the smaller the sum he would cough up. She learned to copy her mother's guile and subservience. To pirouette in front of him in new hardwon outfits and thank him extravagantly. The only time she kissed him was when he bought her something. A victory kiss.

Her mother made her lie to him about the cost of things and hand her the surplus. It was one of the woman's strategies for acquiring money for herself.

Caroline identified sometimes with <u>Salome</u> in her Bible picture stories with its illustration of the princess, her body glowing through demure powder pink tulle, as she extended golden arms to receive her prize, the saint's head on a platter. Caroline had drawn him a halo of parsley. Her sympathies lay with Salome despite her face of pure sweaty evil, her tigerish teeth, the hint of sexual fever in the eyes and the curve of the mouth. Why did she get the blame? It was Herod who made her dance; it was Herodias who made her ask for the man's head!

But of course Caroline's father was nothing like the royal terrorist. Nothing so outrageous. 'Sensible' and 'reasonable' were his favourite words. To him, wisdom was the loss or absence of ideals. He scuttled through life augmenting his income and his dislikes. He did not like blacks, trade unionists, or unmarried mothers, but he would never stone them in the streets.

Caroline loved to read about wonders. Babies born with two heads. Houses whipped a hundred feet into the air in Tornado Alley. Showers of frogs or flowers from the skies. The world was bigger than he dreamed and very unreasonable.

She tried to keep quiet and steer clear of him. Maybe she was too quiet.

One August day just after Caroline's eleventh birthday, she found herself a place on the windowsill of her parents' bedroom. She wanted to sketch the apple tree in the garden, its abundance of leaves and the great cidery mulch of fallen fruit at its base. She could not capture the dancing green light. Her crayons produced only flat blocks of colour. Her father's car appeared in the driveway. Thursday. His half day. She was glad that she had already eaten lunch, and went on humming and drawing. After a while, voices and feet on the stairs. Both her parents entered the room. Caroline was sheltered from view by the curtain.

'Where has she taken herself off to?' he asked.

'I don't know. She never says, little gadabout!' Caroline froze. Why the grudge in her mother's voice? What had she done wrong?

'Good to get rid of her sometimes, eh?'

'You hardly ever see her!'

Caroline started to shake. She could not announce herself now. She did not want to hear any more. 'Go away, go away, I want rid of *you*!' she prayed.

Rustling and fumbling, shoes falling on the floor. They were changing to go out, the gadabouts!

'I have something in the oven,' Rita's worried voice. He laughed inordinately at that.

Creaking of the bed. An unearthly silence, then a struggle ensued. Cooing, groans, frightful panting. They sounded like dying beggars. Caroline guessed that they were trying to make a baby. Why did it take so long? Her back was hunched and aching. Sweat broke out on her brow.

A shriek. 'There. Look! That shadow!'

He was bounding across the floor, the curtain was wrenched aside. He gaped at her as if she were a new form of life. She stared back at his body, the lustrous brown bush at his groin, his pale purple stem. A new smell surrounded him, a high briny odour. The most terrifying thing

37

about him was his face. Rita rose from the bed, an indignant bulk. Shock made her limbs clumsy but clarified the look in her eyes. She was radiant with hate.

'Spy! Vicious little spy!'

'Rita. . .' he tried to appease her.

'Get her out of here! Out! Out!'

He began to shoo Caroline away. She moved backwards to the door. Her instinct was that he would not strike her or lay a hand on her while he was bare.

Rita and Gus stayed in their violated chamber, muttering, a council of war.

When they emerged, they were dressed fussily, almost formally. Rita had even fastened a brooch at her throat. Hisses in the kitchen. Finally, an edict. 'You are never to enter our bedroom again. Under any circumstances. Understand?'

Heavy injured silence at dinner.

The incident was never mentioned again but retained its power to coat their faces with embarrassment, halt their tongues in mid-speech. Like once when Caroline suggested a game of 'I Spy' during a car journey, another time when she was suffering from a cold and her mother insisted on rubbing camphor into her chest. Caroline's breasts had started to grow. She felt as if a misdemeanour were being uncovered.

Puberty shamed her. She wanted to hold on to her flat body. She promised herself she would never marry, never enlist in some hallowed union of hairy substantial bodies grunting on top of an eiderdown. She turned beautiful, with blonde hair and long legs, beacons to a blur of young men who tried to woo or intimidate her. Their ordinariness could not tempt her.

Most of her friends claimed or flaunted experience. The important thing to them, Caroline realised, was not to enjoy sex, but simply to have it. It was a social duty, a sowing of tame oats.

Her own hunger for experience took another route. She was determined to become an actor. Of course the butcher was horrified. What a vain giddy girl! His only child should be a bank clerk, an accountant, a topflight administrator in some go-ahead firm. He could not understand her immunity to the romance of money.

Her talent and will grew in secret, nourished by his opposition.

She left school at eighteen with two undazzling 'A' levels. He forked out the money for a secretarial course. It was fortunate that he preferred cash transactions, distrusting the anaesthetic and spendthrift effect of cheques and credit cards. Caroline took the wad of fivers and enrolled herself into a British Theatre Association workshop. When her treachery came to light, recriminations were cut short by an offer of a part in a play on the Edinburgh fringe, which would count towards her Equity card. Her mother hovered while she packed.

'When will you be back?'

'I don't think I'll base myself here when I return, actually.'

Rita sat on the bed. 'Look, I don't know why Daddy is so against the idea. But you know him!' she laughed loudly. 'I keep telling him you have to get it out of your system.'

'Better take a raincoat, I suppose.'

'I've always thought the world of you, you know.'

'I know my lines already. Word perfect. I know everyone's lines.'

'I always said you were clever.'

' "I dreamed I had a child, and even in the dream I saw it was my life, and it was an idiot, and I ran away. But it crept on to my lap again, clutched at my clothes. Until I thought, if I could kiss it. . ." '

'What's this? You want to have a child?'

'Those are some of my lines, pinhead!'

Rita's eyes grew round like a rebuked child's. 'Perhaps we could drive up and see your performance.'

'Edinburgh is quite a distance, Mum.'

'Not too far for you, though!'

'No.'

They stared at each other. Rita was barring her way.

'Well, darling.'

'Why don't you pluck your eyebrows, Mum? Honest to God. . .'

Exit left.

'Caroline! Caroline! Wait!'

She marched like Orpheus fleeing through the underworld, but with no impulse to look back.

And now her mother and father were dead. They died within months of each other like inseparable lovers. The loss of her father did not distress Caroline: it simply perfected his absence. But when her mother fell ill, she was stricken with panic and grief.

Kidney trouble. Heart trouble. Always a plump woman, her mother's body had fattened alarmingly. Her skin was sallow and purplish as corn-fed chicken. On release from hospital, she instructed her cousin to hire a nurse from some private agency to tend her at home. The nurse was male. Caroline disliked him at first sight. Bill acted like a butler, surly and possessive, full of haughty meekness. He flirted with the invalid, called her 'Princess'. She giggled at his coaxings and compliments. Was this his way of ostracizing Caroline, or did this grotesque behaviour go on all the time, she wondered?

One day there was a smell like rotting hay from Rita's bed.

'Christ, she's peed herself,' Caroline realized. 'He must change her, bathe her. . .' Bill, the noble nurse, cleanser of all that blubber, those oozing orifices! Lack of revulsion was his gift. She thought about Bill a lot; it was a way of not thinking too much about Rita.

How can she stand it? Caroline asked herself. But Rita was supremely happy. The illness was her masterpiece. Bill was her accomplice, sharing her bedsized frozen life, as devoted as she was to the minute recital of her aches and pains, their intensities, variations, and sudden exemptions.

'A rough night, wasn't it, Princess. We saw the dawn rise, didn't we, love?'

He really cares for her, Caroline thought, guilty and awed. No, he can't! Don't prostitutes also feign love for a fee?

Bill and Rita played cards together, ate snacks, and gossiped. Caroline felt always like an interloper. Once she had to flee from the room in tears. Was Bill the only man who had ever touched Rita with loving kindness?

In the middle of summer, Rita collapsed and was rushed to hospital. Caroline experienced the next few days like a dull fever, the taxi rides past the hot hazed gardens, the sales signs in the shop windows: 'Bargain Time! Silly Sale! Last few days!' Money and fashion, how vain and vulgar and frivolous they were, monstrous distractions to hide the fact of death!

She had forgotten about Bill. Dominic sent her round to pay him off. His charge would not be coming home.

Bill tried to hide his tears. 'I'm sorry. You get fond of people. . .' And then they were holding each other. She was leading him up to her old room. Taking comfort from a stranger's tender lust. For the first time.

Next day, Rita opened her eyes once, stared deeply at Caroline, murmured 'Betsy', the name of her pet terrier, and died.

She was sixty-two.

Was her life long or short? Caroline wondered.

★

Caroline did not weep, but for months after the funeral she went into an unshakeable lethargy. Even speech was difficult. Dominic grew irritable.

'It's not as if there was any love lost between you! An accident of birth made her your mother. So what? There was no resemblance between you of body or mind. . . It's just some kind of conformist piety that's making you act like this!'

'You're right, I didn't love her. That's what makes it so hard. Oh, why don't you help me, Dominic.'

He mellowed, unable to resist a direct appeal. 'Of course, I'll help you! Tell me what to do!'

'I don't know.'

He kissed her softly. 'It'll be all right. Anyway, I know you. You thrive on adversity!'

Caroline gained weight. She went on the Scarsdale Diet. No difference. The Beverly Hills Diet gave her diarrhoea and a blistered mouth from eating too much pineapple. In two hours she regained the two pounds she had lost. The Weight Watchers eating plan added another four pounds. Jogging round the block made her faint. She was turning into fat like her mother! Pink ballooning flesh. Uncontrollable. It was as if a new large body were surrounding her with its ghostly contours, waiting for her to fill it. She began to eat furtively, standing beside the fridge cramming food into her mouth. She forced herself to vomit every day. It made her feel light and free and crafty. She had no choice. After all, she had tried everything else.

She turned her back on Dominic every night, afraid of reeking stomach juices into his face. But then she read an article on bulimia nervosa and learned that habitual vomiting strips enamel from the teeth, destroys the stomach, liver, and kidneys, causes malnutrition and even death. Some days she refrained from the habit, just to prove that she was still in control, could give up when she wanted. But the urge haunted her, even when she succeeded.

She enrolled in a therapy group for eating disorders. Some of her fellow sufferers thought that eating itself was a disorder. The therapist was a man. The disorderly eaters were all women. They included an acupuncturist, a bookshop owner, a textile designer, a stepmother, a Brazilian poet, secretaries, and students, but Caroline could not remember which biography belonged to which face. She could not even remember their names. All distinctions faded except size and

41

age. Here as elsewhere, power and volubility belonged to the thin. Whole lives were dedicated to the defeat of appetite, to the meticulous recording in special notebooks of every bite ingested (for those who had not quit ingesting!). The women listened passionately to stories of struggle and surrender: 'And then I had a baked potato, only a medium size, with a little smidgeon of cheese, and a diet Coke, and then I just had to have a bowl of muesli. I sprinkled a lot of bran on, but. . .' The therapist was slender. 'I haven't always been like this!' he apologized. His forehead was pearled with the sweat of sympathy. A kindly evangelist.

'If you are using food as a comfort, a substitute, to allay or assuage emotion, my friends, you know and I know that it will never work!'

Nods and murmurs from the congregation.

'You might as well have a hole in the back of your neck! You have to discover what it is in you that is crying out for nourishment.'

Caroline looked around her. What did they lack? What did she lack? These women had husbands, lovers, children, homes, careers, money, beauty. . . Why weren't they all bloated with fulfilment?

'Satisfaction!' the therapist was saying fervently. Had she missed The Answer? He talked on about Heart and Will and Purpose. Caroline was regretting her cheque. He would probably start enthusing about God in a minute. ('Yes Lord! He can Satisfy!') Your unporky Saviour. Star of the Least Supper. The softly chiding voice started to relate a dire warning story. A girl with chronic bulimia became dangerously underweight and was taken forcibly to hospital. The medical staff placed her in a side ward and accompanied her on visits to the toilet. She was watched at meal times to make sure that she ate the food. Still, her weight did not alter. The doctors were extremely worried and perplexed. Eventually they discovered a suitcase full of vomit under the girl's bed. Caroline looked around to see the effect of this homily. Gleam of triumph on many a gaunt face! Clever girl to outwit the tyrants who would forcefeed her! They were mentally adding her stratagem to their emergency repertoire. Vomit did not disgust them. It was a necessary process in the art of starvation. Did the crushed insects, ground to create a beautiful shade of red, disgust Titian? The evening ended with an affirmative chant. The women stood and chorused:

'My body is ideal for me right now!'

'Louder! Louder!' the therapist harangued them.

'My body is ideal for me right now!'

'As if you mean it!'
'*My body is ideal for me right now!*'
Caroline burst into tears.

'Don't touch her!' he commanded. Solicitous hands were withdrawn. She heard him muttering about 'catharsis', 'unleashing of painful emotion', 'breakthrough'. Respectful covetous eyes were trained on her. She swallowed her curative tears. Too much was expected of them. She went home and started wailing again. Her 'hysteria' panicked Dominic into calling the doctor.

'Do you really not know what's wrong with you?' Dr Lomax smiled.

'I'm depressed. I'm putting on weight even though I eat practically nothing.'

'When did you last have a period?'

'Oh!'

Next day it was confirmed. Four months pregnant! She decided that Dominic was, must be, the father. She stopped vomiting. Started eating for two or three. What if the baby were malnourished? Irremediably damaged?

Worry and relief took turns. The extra weight wasn't herself, it was the baby. She imagined him as a sort of swelling tapeworm.

Dominic was gleeful at the prospect of fatherhood. She suspected that he welcomed the baby as proof to the outside world of their marital passion. Who would guess now that they copulated once a season, usually in their sleep? He pampered Caroline, invented a dozen pet names for her, plied her with gifts. Shame inspired her to a bright public gaiety. Heads turned at her rosy cheeks and shining eyes. Her body was celebrating, even if she could not. Sometimes her happiness felt real. Was she acting with such conviction that even she. . .? She started to notice babies and toddlers in the street, in gardens, in supermarkets, an unfathomable race of pygmies who had been invisible to her before. She didn't want a baby. Didn't want that endless passionate involvement. Alone in her room, she gave way to terror, choking with tears, rocking back and forth, wringing her hands. She had performed such antics many times. Stage tricks. So it made her uneasy when they happened to her in reality. Insincere. Besides, these gestures gave no relief. How could there be any relief? The baby was there, inside, growing, and that was that. Bow down to nature and breed.

Alasdair was only six weeks old when Caroline started to hire babysitters every other afternoon. She told them she was going to yoga classes, the dentist's, or the doctor's. But really she was just wandering about, pretending to be free. She never told Fran that she had watched her often in the park before she plucked up courage to speak. Fran sat every afternoon alone and engrossed, as if her mind were flooding with dreams. Caroline was drawn by this atmosphere of undreary calm. The woman's eyes were beautiful and untroubled but not dim, not at all. Perhaps Caroline hoped to catch serenity from her or at least discover its source. And so everything began.

'What part of Scotland are you from?' Caroline had asked after a few moments' conversation, confident that she recognised the accent.

Fran grinned. 'The far west.'

'Ayrshire?'

'I'm from Belfast.'

Caroline realised very soon that Fran's imperturbable air was the result of trauma and monstrous loneliness. She was jolted by questions about her pregnancy as if the fact of her condition had forcibly caught her attention for the first time. When Caroline touched her sleeve lightly, Fran flinched. Then in embarrassment she tried to cancel the rebuff by moving closer. In the tearoom she relaxed and talked dispassionately about herself as if she were reading out a coroner's report on someone else. How odd to listen to her cautious elegant phrases outlining a life apparently out of her control! She sounded like some natural misfit with a 'useless' degree and a whole string of both posh and menial jobs behind her. The distinction was Caroline's: Fran despised all her 'servitudes' equally. She became restless in employment, she said, and either left impulsively or managed to get herself thrown out.

'I was sacked from my last job for insubordination and fractious behaviour.'

'Sounds like expulsion from a boarding school!' Caroline laughed uneasily. It was hard to imagine Fran anarchic and driven. She had the cold charisma of a Chinese empress.

'More like prison,' she said. ' "Earning a living." I hate that expression! Your life in exchange for your living!'

'What do you do with your time now?'

Fran blushed. 'Waste it! I stopped them robbing me of my time. Now I rob myself.'

'My time,' Caroline murmured. 'I never think of time belonging to me in that way. What would you like to do?'

'Now or in general?'

'With *your* time?'

She shrugged. 'I'd love a long rest. In a convent. A sort of convent for atheists.'

'No men?'

'Men!' Fran said with that air of resigned superiority women assume at such moments and yet it bothered Caroline, disturbed some buried seam of feeling in her.

'There's no tea left,' she said. 'Let's order some more.'

Fran lifted the lid and peered inside the empty pot.

'Don't you believe me?'

'Oh yes, of course I do. I don't know why I did that.'

'Very suspicious.'

Strange how swiftly they became close friends: neither was used to friendship. Maybe it was childbearing that did it. They had already been invaded, were already sharing themselves richly. Why hold back?

4

Emily

Fran

We hammered it out, Caroline and I. We agreed that I should move into their house at once. After the birth, we would share child care for six weeks or longer if I were not fully recovered. Then she would pay me forty pounds a week clear for looking after Alasdair and undertaking certain household tasks like preparing the evening meal for all of us. Caroline would be free to attend auditions and take up work. During her 'resting' periods, she would sometimes be around and would help. I was to have two days a week entirely free except when Caroline was acting. Then she would either pay me more or permit me to hire agency staff.

I moved in. I was saved; completely happy. Caroline was always teasing me about my 'bovine bliss'. Dominic annoyed her and embarrassed me with his gleeful anticipation of the birth. As if it were his child!

'You two are so sentimental about children,' Caroline accused us. 'They might be horrible, you do realise? Chopping up worms, dismembering their teddies. They might grow up to be traffic wardens or psychopaths.'

'Traffic wardens are psychopaths,' Dominic said helpfully.

'All the kids we know are maniacs. That horrible little Sebastian who locked his mother in the garage for five hours! And that little angelface Laura! Spends all her time alienating Moira's friends: 'Are you the lady wiv only one bweast? My mummy says you're forty-five if you're a day? Why does your husband sleep in another house at night. . .?'

Dominic threw me a conspiratorial smile: 'Our kids won't be like that, will they, Fran?'

'Oh, our kids won't be like that!' Caroline mimicked him. 'The Mamas and the Papas!'

'I hate that word "kids" ', I said quickly. 'Kids and nannies.'

'You don't look like a nanny to me,' Dominic said.

'Thank God for that!'

'Oh, it's not a compliment coming from him! Our Dominic likes a bit of the strict and starchy. He didn't go to a public school for nothing!'

'Ignore her!' he smiled. 'Anyway, I can't see you devoting yourself completely to nannyhood. What will you do in your spare time?'

'Yes,' said Caroline. 'What will you do?'

'Well, I think I'll work on the cure for cancer and train to be an astronaut.'

'Oh, you'll be able to fit that in easily between nappies. That reminds me, there's this new service, a van that delivers disposable nappies in bulk. . . I've got the leaflet somewhere.'

'What a luxury! I wonder what it says on the van: "Crap Packs"? "Spread the Load"?'

'Here it is! We're going to use them. Hang the expense!'

I laughed. 'You make everything so easy and stylish.'

'You and I are going to turn this motherhood caper into a doddle! No puke stains, furrowed brows, and post-natal brain damage!'

'My mother never recovered from having me. Of course, there were no disposable nappies in those days. No disposable foetuses either.'

'Is it "foetuses" or "foeti", I wonder?' Caroline said. She had a refreshing way of short-circuiting my bad memories.

On the eleventh of November, six days after the date I circled in red, I awoke to find my thighs bathed in the warm amniotic fluid.

'This is it,' I thought. I just wanted to go on lying there, wanted time to suspend itself. But I rose and staggered to the bathroom.

'Caroline!' I yelled.

'Right. I'll get the car out of the garage.' She knew by my tone of voice.

'Shall I stay?' she asked when we reached the ward.

'Yes! No! I don't know!'

'I'm staying,' she decided.

Admission procedure. Undress. Shaving. Enema. Panic-breaths. Contractions, always when I am not ready for them.

'Dear, dear, what a fuss! You'll scare the other patients.'

The shining white coat offers me an injection.

'Yes! No! I don't know!'

Hours of floating, surfacing again and again into red spasms of pain. Medical voices coming at me like an ill-tuned radio.

Suddenly they rip her from me. She cries like a seagull. I am holding her. My dusky girl. Eyes wide and receptive. Hands like anemones.

Tiny cleft vagina, lips perfectly closed. Emily.

5

The Stealer of Light

Caroline

She passed and trespassed through the house, her hands touching everything, asserting possession. Her Celtic melancholy could penetrate walls. She was always holding Alasdair in her arms. Holding him hostage. Intercepting his mother's love. She was like the Moon, Caroline thought. A stealer of light. No, she was a black hole, drawing everything towards her into her crushing gravity. Even Ireland was like a country she had swallowed rather than lived in.

Everything Fran did became an imposition. Her hygiene was selective. The carpets might be knee-deep in crumbs, fluff, and newspapers, but her cleansing furies were directed only at Caroline's rubbish.

Admittedly, Caroline's process of beautification was lazy and obsessive and she did tend to deposit little used cotton wool balls and crumpled Kleenex everywhere. And if she did leave a ring round the bath, whose bath was it, anyway? Fran trailed after Caroline, lifting her detritus, emptying and wiping her ashtrays with all the reproving zeal of the reformed smoker. And with a servant's contempt, Caroline decided. As if she wanted to erase. . .

'We're the usurpers.' She remembered Fran saying that about her own race of Northern Irish Protestants.

'Imagine, I've been here a year already!' Fran chirped one day. 'Can you believe it?'

Oh yes, I can believe it, Caroline thought. Fran also had an ex-salvationist's nostalgia for austerity, which expressed itself occasionally in rigorous diets. When she discovered Macrobiotics, the household was subjected to a fortnight of queasiness. Twice daily feasts of brown rice, stewed pumpkin, and seaweed. She only stopped when Dominic started to bring home Chinese takeaways.

He never lifts an eyebrow to her! Caroline noticed. Totally unremonstrative. He was crazy about her. And she knew how to exploit the romance of her blighted past! Her accent thickened when she was

48

losing an argument. She persisted in a precautionary lifestyle, always varying her routes home, for instance. It might make sense in Belfast, but in London it was just potty to devise such lengthy circuitous changes in her comings and goings. Was it some kind of ritual solidarity with the haunted and hunted citizens of Belfast? Or was it one of her provocative despisals of the English, for their safe existence?

'She has an imaginary pursuer,' Dominic said. 'Haven't you noticed how she keeps looking over her shoulder? Jumps at the rustle of leaves?'

He was charmed by such fragility, of course. And so glad to be providing refuge for a political exile. He assumed she was a Catholic, simply because she took a rather anaemic Republican stance. He wouldn't be so keen if he found out he was harbouring a middle-class Ulster Protestant! About as much glory in that as shacking up with a white South African. It served him right.

Yes, she was hitting it off splendissimo with the Professor!

Like all uneasy immigrants, Fran thirsted for politics. She and Dominic ruined every meal time with their analyses of the latest atrocity here, act of folly there. Their whining reasonable voices would go on and on. The more intractable the problem under discussion, the more freely flowed the refrains of 'Absolutely', 'Clearly', 'Simply', 'Obviously'. Caroline would watch them in silence. Their postures mirrored each other. Their talk was a disguise for something else.

Sometimes they remembered Caroline's existence, and one or other of them would say 'What do you think?' And they would wait, really anxious, as if her word would carry an umpire's weight. Sometimes she short-changed them with a smile. Sometimes she pretended not to have listened.

'About what?'

'Arthur Scargill.'

'Rotten hairdo.'

She would play her allotted role: the ninny. Dumb brunette. She could see relief and scorn spreading over their features. And so they put the world to rights while the central heating purred and the burglar alarm protected their cosy share of it.

Dominic was detached and knowledgeable, citing facts and figures. To him it was all part of the Human Comedy, daft and irremediable. But Fran seemed to care. She wept over the mutilated Falklands veterans. Picketed the South African embassy. Visited Greenham Common. Poured Superglue into the keyholes of porn shops. She had a kind of creative suffering, always seeking new occasions, new discomforts. The chip on her shoulder was the size of the Mountains of Mourne!

'I do think Irish people are well integrated and accepted in this country,' Caroline dared to say one day.

Fran launched into a barrage of anti-Irish jokes, meticulous and unabridged: 'What do you do if an Irish man throws a pin at you? Run, he has a grenade in his mouth. Why did the Irish novelist call himself Ball Point? His publisher told him to use a pen-name. . .'

On and on with perfect recall, like Gulliver removing stickpins from his flesh one by one.

'Hear about the Irish rapist who tied his victim's legs together so that she could not run away. . .?'

'OK, OK, they're not very funny. But they're harmless,' Caroline said without much conviction. The speed and intensity of Fran's delivery, or perhaps the sheer quantity of the jokes, did give them a malevolent ring.

'Harmless! Oh sure! They express and perpetuate the belief that we're just a bunch of subhuman Paddies, so who cares what happens to us? Just a bunch of thick Paddies. Thick! Thick! Thick! Or as Paddy would say: T'ick, t'ick, t'ick! That's good, isn't it? The sound of a primed bomb!'

The more Caroline resented Fran, the more she feared her. The details, which emerged gradually, of Fran's 'affair' with Emily's father made Caroline recoil. How could she have been so shockingly passive? Why had she not sought an abortion? It must have been Fran's calm fatalism that had made her drift along. Her body had a kind of peasant effectuality about it, that was almost a liability. She would more easily be moved to violence than to any kind of flight.

You lack panic, Caroline thought. No gift of panic.

And yet Fran joked that her name was short for 'Frantic', and it was eerily true. She was phlegmatic and powerful. Her deep subterranean fury only rarely surfaced, but there was a disturbance in the air around her. A kind of endogenous rage behind the gentleness like a revolver tucked inside a lady's muff. Dominic sensed this too, but he constructed a romance round it. He showed Caroline a book one day: *Who Killed Charles Bravo?*, a true-life Victorian murder mystery.

'Look at this picture,' he said. 'It's Florence Bravo, the lovely poisoner. Spitting image of our Fran, isn't it?' And there was Fran, same cow-eyed chilling innocence, same dreamy oval face, sensuous mouth. Only the dress and hairstyle were different.

Dominic doted on Emily also. The seraphic Emily. On trips to the shops or park at weekends it was always Emily he wanted to carry. His little black albatross. Alasdair was puny and plaintive, the vehicle of his mother's fear. He and Caroline were the also-rans in Dominic's affection.

'But life isn't a *Dallas* script, you know!' Dominic was saying as Caroline entered the kitchen.

'I know, but I can't stand those sort of books. . .'

O God! Caroline thought. Literary debates at dawn!

'Why?'

'You know, all those "small moments"! The faithful itemisation of tiny sensation: "I had an eggnog before lying down to listen to some Haydn. The sky was blue. The windows needed washing. Shortly after nine o'clock the postman delivered the mail. Three circulars, the gas bill, and a postcard from Uncle Ralph who was spending his male menopause in Miami".'

Dominic laughed. 'But don't you see, there's always something going on underneath the banal coating?'

Caroline intervened: 'How very true!'

The phone rang. Everyone stiffened but no one moved. Caroline had long since stopped climbing out of bed, bath or black mood to answer the phone because it was always for Dominic. That much sought after person now cocked his head beseechingly at Fran and she trotted off happily. 'Don't forget. I'm not here!' he called after her.

'Isn't she useful?' he said friendlily. 'And so bright!'

Caroline spooned some egg yolk into her mouth.

'I'm trying to persuade her to do a part-time higher degree. She shows such promise, don't you think?'

Promise. Such a sexual word, Caroline thought. Promiscuous.

She could easily feel sorry for Fran. She knew Dominic's technique. His careful blend of control and congratulation. And when he lost interest in Fran, she would be like Caroline now: Cinderella at midnight.

'You know, Dominic, if you were a woman, no one would seek your approval.'

'How wonderful it must be. To be a woman,' he sighed. Fran came back into the room.

'Who was it?'

'Don't know. She didn't give her name.'

'O God, it might have been important. I'll worry all day now!'

'I'm awfully sorry. . .'

'O God, can't delegate anything safely.'

As he departed he blew a kiss at Fran and tapped Caroline on the bum. Some subtle signalling of their respective places in his caste system.

The two women became immediately silent and tense in his absence.

'I'll clear up breakfast,' Fran muttered.

'Leave it!'

'What?'

'Bloody leave it! . . . You can have him if you want.'

'What? What are you talking about?'

' "Have" him. "Have" as in "fuck".'

'You've got the wrong idea, Caroline! I wouldn't dream of trying to damage your marriage.'

'What marriage? There is no marriage!'

'Caroline, sometimes it takes a long time to get back to normal after having a baby. . .'

'We are back to normality. Back to nullity.'

'It can't be that bad.'

'Can't it?'

She took Fran by the wrist and led her into the lounge, unlocked the bureau drawer and removed her folder. Spread its contents on the table. Letters, cards, poems, photographs from the men who answered Caroline's 'Lonely Hearts' advertisements. Their replies ranged from scraps of paper with little more than a phone number scribbled on them to fifteen page autobiographies. Fran lifted one or two at random, read them white-faced. She left the room without a word.

6

Lonely Hearts

Fran

Are you my dream? Man, young 49, seeks uncomplicated damsel for fun, fantasy, and frolics. PHOTO ESSENTIAL.

Successful solvent male wants to meet slender unopinionated Venus in blue jeans. Must be discreet.

Guy, thirties, needs broadminded buxom lady.

Cuddly woman, sense of humour, own home, lotta love, seeks male companion.

Lively independent woman seeks nice guy for laughs and loving times.

Four things struck me about these mating calls:

1. Men stipulated their requirements.
2. Women displayed their wares.
3. There was a habit of alliteration in their composition: 'cuddly caring', 'sensual slim sensitive sincere', 'gorgeous groovy gal', 'large-breasted lovelies', 'lissom libertine'.
4. This was how Caroline found her lovers!

For weeks after her revelation, we did not allude to it. But then she became tired of my suspicious reaction every time she claimed to be going to an audition.

'Don't look at me like that, Fran! Meetings with prospective lovers are a kind of audition!'

'I'd rather you didn't lie to me, that's all. After all, it was your decision to impose your secret on me!'

'As you like.'

From then onwards, she disclosed more and more. It seemed to relieve and amuse her to talk about her tacky loves. She claimed that most of her 'applicants' were 'satisfactory', not the wimps, freaks, and untouchables of my imagination. In fact, the men she selected for a few bouts of coitus sounded just like her: beautiful, sanitary, discreetly talented. Civilised predators with manicured claws. Of course, she also met quite a few duds 'n' deadheads on her diligent dates. There was the hapless Roy, who sounded so good on paper. Born hopelessly under Cancer, he turned out to be six feet four of hypochondriac enfeeblement. Plump moon-face, wet pink lips, quilted anorak, a pipe constantly in need of investigating, reloading, relighting, all things despised by the lovely Caroline. He treated her to a trudge round Streatham before they retired to his bedsit for a drink of Barleycup. Every inch of wall was plastered with tits, bums, and moist pubes. Bits of Woman, like the mounted stags' heads in the home of the hunter to remind him and everyone, lest they doubt it, that he is indeed the victor, the possessor. Caroline felt queasy. Could this great senile baby have desires? Designs? Roy the Boy sat hugely on the floor and offered her a catarrh pastille.

'No thanks.'

'I suck them all year round,' he said proudly. 'Even in summer.'

Caroline made her excuses and fled from the den of masturbation, refusing the offer of an escort through Muggerland.

Then there was Otto the Author, a Woody Allen look-alike minus the wit. He sat all evening in the 'Hare and Hounds' lubricating his monologue with gulps of tomato juice, which supplied the only pauses. He confessed to having published a pamphlet on the history of badminton, but preferred to relate the entire plots of his three unwritten novels.

Outside, he suggested taking a short cut across Hampstead Heath. Caroline wondered later if he had said a 'short rut'. He became lyrical about their stupendous affinity of soul. 'We've so much in common, isn't it amazing? And you're exceptionally beautiful and intelligent. Most females are negligible, I can tell you frankly. . .'

He whipped off his glasses and pulled her towards him, began his frantic damp attentions. She couldn't stop him for laughing. However, this meeting of true minds was prevented by a fleshy hitch.

'You don't arouse me enough,' he pronounced. 'Beautiful women just aren't sensual. You think you don't have to try.'

'Thank God you have at least one unswollen part,' Caroline told him.

'Why bother?' I asked her once when she was voluble with complaints about her 'misadventures'.

'Sometimes I get lucky, that's why.'

'Laughs, lust, libido, lasciviousness, liquory lecherous liaisons.'

'Yes please.'

'But never love?'

'No fear! You'd like that, wouldn't you? To see me doing penance. Disinfecting my peccadilloes with a shower of tears.'

'What do you get out of it?'

She laughed nastily.

'OK, apart from the obvious?'

'I'll tell you. The shock of a new body! Wondering what a man will say or do. Not knowing it all by heart. I like men to make an effort to please me. I'm not a dispenser of tea and therapy! I don't want to nurse any egos. Maybe I'm no good at being a wife. But I'm a bloody brilliant peripatetic mistress!'

She pulled back a strand of her hair, which crackled with electricity. Her eyes were full of a kind of anger, or was it just her restless spendthrift energy?

'Your Olympic fucking depresses me.'

'Oh yes?'

'It's all so heartless and soulless. What a pity you and your bedmates can't unzip your genitals and let them lead their own merry dance without dragging the rest of you in tow.'

'Don't give me any of your New Puritan sermons! God knows, it must be the only fashionable thing about you!'

That hurt. So I was unfashionable apart from my trendy celibacy. Unpassionable. A marginal person. It occurred to me more and more that Caroline's amorous vocation depended upon me fulfilling the despised roles of Mother, Housekeeper, even Wife. I spent more time with Dominic than she did. My annoyance increased when Caroline landed a part in a Restoration comedy. She played a high-minded but beleaguered virgin. At home she practised her lines on me. I was amazed at her transformation into an ethereal angel, unacquainted and undisturbed by carnal knowledge. I was sick of being sad, drab, and harmless to know.

The first thing Dominic did each day when he returned home was to pour us both a drink.

'Let's get rid of the *bambini*,' he said one noisy fractious evening.

'I would, but it's against the law.'

'I mean, a quick despatch cotwards.'

We fitted the squealing wriggling infants into the bathtub together and washed one body each. The chore became fun as the babies calmed down and the warm smell of soap rose and surrounded us. Our fingers kept colliding in the water when we searched for the soap. I became silent watching Dominic's hands as he cradled my Emily, as he scooped her up in a towel.

The babies did not resist being put to bed. Emily fell asleep at once. Alasdair lay in sweet contemplation.

'Just look at them,' Dominic whispered. They were heartbreakingly beautiful and vulnerable.

'What will happen to them?' I said in a sudden seizure of panic.

'Boredom, I suppose, at the very least.' And then, as if the thought were too oppressive, he spoke briskly: 'Come on, let's retire to the study.'

I sat on the window-seat as Dominic selected and poured our large tipples.

'I'll be held in here like a hostage until *she* appears,' I thought. For a split second, I felt like saying 'I have things to do, you know, exercises, assignations, prayers, anything. . .'

But he would just switch on his adamant smile: 'What's your hurry? Don't you have plenty of leisure? A Room of Your Own? A little Life of Your Own?'

Yes. Yes. So did Bertha Rochester.

I stared resentfully at Dominic's back. Dominic of Dominic and Caro. I was nothing but the silent register of the seismic shifts of their marriage. Their moody subliminal combat that soaked up all our energies like greedy flowers in a sickroom. I knew but did not understand about his long walks at night, his consoling drinks. I knew but did not understand about her rising at dawn to walk barefoot in the garden. There was his deliberate ignoring of the phone ringing; her off-key singing while he scribbled lecture notes at breakfast. His fraternal kisses on her forehead, exactly at the hairline; her 'forgetting' to call him down for lunch. His migraines; her backache. His compliments and courtesies towards me, her shrug calculated to hurt, her failure to deliver the blow. Their quarrels about the baby instead of . . . what?

I overheard snatches of accusing dialogue:

She: How mean and nasty you can be!

He: Sorry, I didn't intend. . .

She: Don't act stupid! You've been perfecting your malice for years.

He: Well, some of us have to work at it!

Dominic was in front of me proffering the brandy.

'Why are you so unhappy?' I blurted out, reckless before even one sip of alcohol.

He laughed: 'I love it in here, don't you? My quiet immaculate study.'

He raised his glass in a toast: 'Here's to oblivion! To bliss, in other words!'

'Oblivion can't be bliss. You're not present to enjoy it!'

'You remind me of my most irritating student, Robin Freeman. It's a matter of tireless conscience with him to contradict my every statement, even if it's only "Good morning".'

'Oh, right, I'll go away if I annoy you.'

'Don't sulk. He's a Genius.'

'So, aren't you glad to have a bright student?'

'Not when he's demonstrably brighter than me!'

'You're always complaining about how dull it is to teach the docile mediocrities, how sick it makes you to see your own opinions swallowed without suspicion and repeated in thirty different scrawls!'

'Reverently, inelegantly, and illegibly repeated!'

I passed my hand over my eyes in mockery of Dominic's habitual melancholy gesture: ' "Jesus, those dim little doxies, those trying-hard no-hopers!" Quote. Unquote.' He had finished his drink already, so I poured him another brandy.

'Oh thanks, thanks,' he said, caressing the bulb of the glass as if it were conscious. He went on ruefully: 'I made the mistake of assuming that a gifted student would appreciate my well-stocked mind! But Freeman despises me. Mimics my words, all the little phrases I've leaned on: "quality of life", "spiritual dimension", "personal freedom", "the creative individual". He makes me sound like . . . feel like a fat ratepayer! He dismisses most of the authors on the course: "that cow with her febrile intensity", "that brothel creeper with his nursery rhymes". But he writes like an angel, a scourging angel with an IQ of a hundred and eighty. Of course he's wrong sometimes, but even when he's wrong, he's more right than me! Sure, he uses his knowledge like a weapon, but how do I use mine? As a social grace, a mantle of respectability. . .'

'A meal ticket,' I added helpfully.

'So you see, every day I hope he won't come, but when he doesn't I really miss him and his jagged comments and I worry like hell in case he's staying away *deliberately*. And I have to cut short the class, because I can't stand those tame acquiescent faces, that cartload of chameleons all faded to the most neutral uniform shabby shade possible. . . It's like preparing to negotiate a minefield and finding yourself in a meadow.'

'A habit of insult doesn't make a genius,' I said.

'No, but it helps. He resists all contamination except his own.'

'What does he look like, this prodigy? Robin is such a sweety-lamb name!'

'Like an elderly man with a child's face. Specs. Hunched shoulders. Asthma. Fierce and friendless. He reminds me of you a little,' he said, looking at me closely. 'There's something stinging and demonic about both of you.'

I started to tremble, distressed at this incidental judgement of me delivered with such diagnostic composure. I wanted to say: 'Don't compare me with some miserable boy! Don't sum me up. Don't imagine that you know. . .' But I knew that Dominic wasn't interested in me now. All his thoughts were with the Boy Wonder.

Once again, my glass was replenished. I could smell the liquor on Dominic's breath. The room was darkening. Was it eight o'clock? Nine o'clock? I heard a sound of running liquid.

'Oops,' he laughed, pointing to my glass which I was unknowingly holding tilted.

'God, there's no sensation in my fingers! Oh, I'll have to wipe the carpet.'

'Leave it, leave it.'

'What will you do about him, about Robin?' I asked, without interest.

He spoke in a tender brooding voice, as if to himself. 'I'd like to take him in my arms. Yes, I'd like to take his poor loveless brain-polluted body in my arms.'

I kept my voice steady: 'And will you?'

'Oh, Jesus, no, I never do anything . . . extravagant. I'm not real, you know. Unlike you.'

'Me?'

'Yes, you wanted a baby, so you damn well had a baby and to hell with the obstacles.'

'No, I did not want her! It wasn't like that. I could feel her or I could imagine her wanting herself. She was accidentally in me, not belonging to me, just in me and longing to be. . . And I let her. But so long as she lives, so does the event that brought her into being. I'm connected crazily to a man, to a past I despise.'

He wasn't listening.

58

'You know, I love Alasdair and Emily, but I can't quite believe in them. Do you know what I mean? I can hardly credit that I gave them their lives.'

'You didn't give Emily her life,' I reminded him gently.

'I like your teeth,' he said, 'sort of translucent, with weak enamel like the teeth of an unhealthy person. Don't look away: it's an endearing little defect in your beautiful head. Did I ever tell you about Franz Kafka?'

'I know about Kafka,' I said angrily, with maximum dental concealment.

'He died a happy man.'

'He died in agony from tuberculosis, unable to speak. He died far too young.'

'Don't impose your feeling on him! He said that the earliest spot on his lung was the "first sign of health". He said that his suffering had purchased his freedom from his parents, his fiancée, his job, all the strictures of his life!'

'That's horrific!'

'Why?'

'God, I don't want to taste freedom for the first time on my deathbed!'

'Fine. Be free. Run wild. I'll watch. I'm an old academic. Second-hand experience is my speciality.' The brandy bottle was almost empty.

'The booze helps you in that, doesn't it? Paralyses the springs of action.'

He sang suddenly:
    ' "Here we go round the prickly pear
      The prickly pear the prickly pear
      Here we go round the prickly pear
      At five o'clock in the morning".'

'That's from T. S. Eliot, isn't it?'

'He had a mad wife,' Dominic said.

'A *sad* wife.'

'He wasn't exactly jumping for joy either.'

'Dominic, do you have affairs?'

He laughed: 'I never know whether it's more shameful to say "yes" or "no" to that question!'

'I think perhaps you don't make love with any one.' A sharp intake of breath, then he paid me back in full: 'Only with myself.'

'I'm sorry.'

'For what? Your intrusiveness or my onanistic recourse?'

'I didn't mean to hurt you.'

He grinned suddenly: 'At least your weapons are all visible.'

I kneeled on the window seat to look at the sky. No stars were visible, only the crescent moon.

Dominic turned me round to face him. I had the feeling of skidding down a hill. There was no firmness to his kisses at first. He was like someone in the dark at a party who knows for sure that he will drive home soon with his wife.

But his personality changed when we sank to the floor. We removed our own clothes, so avoiding those fumbling ineptitudes which inspire second thoughts. Speedy reconnaissance of each other, easy slippery convergence.

I was filled with absurd joy at the scarcely formulated idea that now I was really part of the family. Now I could make my full contribution to the household's bitter and deceptive warfare. At the same time, a thousand worries were besieging, eroding, clustering round my happiness like sperm surrounding an egg.

'God, what if Caroline walks in? Jesus, don't let me . . . not another baby . . . Dominic, open your eyes . . . maybe he's so drunk . . . it's me, you know, not Caroline, not your vituperative boy genius. . . What will you do tomorrow? My suitcases in the hall? Frigid civility? Pretend it didn't happen? Forget?'

But oh, it was happening and happening. We were toiling on the tasteful carpet, my real feet crossed at his real sacrum, gripping him in a vice. Nothing false, nothing banned between us any more.

We lay slumped and surprised afterwards, until he spoke: 'I'm getting dreadfully nervous.'

'I know. Better clear up, I suppose.'

We staggered to the vertical. My clothes didn't seem to fit me now. Dominic led me to my room, set me on the bed and patted me.

'You can go now,' I said.

He gave me a chaste kiss. His shirt grazed my arm and that sensation or its echo lingered for hours, as if my skin had a memory of its own.

I couldn't sleep. Life had caught up with me. Messy, lawless life.

7

Family Planning

Fran

At the Family Planning Clinic, the supplies section was separated from the seating area by a screen, permitting every word of donor and recipient to be heard. One woman wailed about her ration of ten condoms per month.

'You've got to be joking! I'm married to a bloke, not a bloody panda!'

Much clearing of throat by the clerk: 'I'm sorry, but we have to give everyone the same amount. It's not arbitrary, you know, that figure is based on statistical research, the average number of time couples er. . .'

'Where'd you find these couples? Bognor Regis?'

'That's all I can give you, I'm afraid!' Sound of boxes being slapped on to the desk.

'Look here! Women who take the pill or have one of them wire things, they're protected at all times, right? At all times, day and night. Well, you're refusing to protect me at all times. It's discrimination.'

'You could opt for the pill or the intra-uterine device if you're not satisfied with your present method, Mrs ah. . .'

'The pill made me pregnant. The coil made me haemorrhage. The cap bounced all over the bathroom floor.' But the keeper of the sheaths stood firm and the poor woman had to stomp off.

The next client explained her embarrassment at the nasty pong of her Dutch cap.

'It reeks right after use! It's like a dead mackerel. And if I can smell it, so can everyone! I keep wanting to remove it before the six hours.'

'It's a problem some people experience, I'm afraid, especially in hot weather. Not a lot you can do, really. Try dusting it with a little talcum powder after cleaning.'

Don't do that! I thought. Talc is carcinogenic. I had read so in some authoritative scary journal. Should I warn her? But smegma is carcinogenic. Breathing is probaby carcinogenic. I couldn't save her.

I was feeling discouraged. The prevention business had obviously not advanced much since I last availed myself of its paraphernalia. I distrusted the pill and the intra-uterine device. It would have to be rubber and goo. I remembered their respective odours. Why did no one think of inventing banana-flavoured spermicide? Or peppermint? Or Cointreau? Maybe I should calculate my fertile periods by temperature charts, by the phases of the moon? Maybe I should spit in a frog's mouth like those seventeenth century women. It would be less troublesome, and more pleasant. I was handed a questionnaire to complete. A long list of queries about children born live or dead, abortions legal or illegal, venereal diseases. A blackmailer's dream.

My turn at last. A woman doctor, bouffant silver hair, creased forehead.

'I need a morning-after pill,' I confessed.

'Slipped up, have we?' she said aptly. 'When was your last period?'

'Oh, I don't know.'

'You have had one recently?'

'Yes . . . but I . . .'

She passed me a calendar: 'Work it out.'

When the hell was it? There was the night Dominic came home from a Marina Tsvetayeva poetry reading, crackling with rapturous quotes, and I responded with as much verve as I would to a parking ticket. But was that the first day or the middle? And what was the date, anyway?

'I'm sorry. I can't recollect it at all.'

'How am I supposed to pinpoint where you are in your cycle? I don't like prescribing these high-dose hormones, they're a desperate remedy, you know.' She began to read my notes: 'Single parent, one termination. . .'

Her eyes gleamed at me: Feckless!

'What contraception do you use?'

'Nothing.'

She looked perturbed.

'I mean, there's been no need.'

'No ne-ed?' she said trisyllabically.

'I didn't. . . I wasn't involved in any relationships.'

'Oh dear!' It was as if I had admitted to some gross dereliction of duty.

She tried to persuade me to take the pill, extolling its convenience, its safety. Either she was in the pay of a pharmaceutical company or she thought that with my 'record', I should be chemically sterilised.

'I see the coil is contra-indicated, as you've had salpingitis in the past. Doesn't leave us with a lot of scope, does it?'

She showed me her array of plastic and copper coils, caps that looked like swollen blisters, sheaths packed in blue boxes and coyly named 'Forget Me Nots'. I imagined presenting Dominic with these items: it seemed an insufficiently lyrical gesture.

'I'd like to be fitted for a cap.' I tried to sound enthusiastic.

'Hm, I had to use one of those. My sons are twenty, eighteen, and thirteen. I didn't want children. Get on the couch.'

She stabbed me with her speculum, then inserted a cap, made me feel it in the correct and incorrect position. I swore blind I could tell the difference.

Then she left me alone with a diagram of the pelvis and instructions to practise insertion and removal until I was a dab hand at it.

The diagram bore no resemblance to the warm damp strangely ridged interior of myself. The cap had a mind of its own. It flew out of my hand. When captured and pointed at its destination, it expanded at the wrong moment. After several futile attempts, my legs ached from squatting. I looked the fugitive rubber in the eye, squeezed it and jammed it in. A triumph of the human will. But then I couldn't get it out. It simply would not emerge! God, they'll have to operate! I thought. I started to cry. The doctor put her head round the door.

'How are we getting on?'

'It won't come out!'

'Course it will.' She disappeared, full of job satisfaction.

I cried some more. What the hell was I doing with my life? How could I allow myself to become a married man's Wet Dream? How could I jeopardize my peace of mind? The roof over my bed?

'I give up on you,' I told myself. 'Ruining your life is your only talent.'

All the loose ends in my existence lined up to reproach me: the fluff under the bed, the half-read novels and self-help manuals, the notebooks stuffed with unrelated scraps of ideas for the Book I Will Definitely Write One Day Not Now. My fingers turned vicious and nimble and I yanked the cap out in one go.

'Who needs you?' I hissed at it.

The doctor came back and insisted that I demonstrate my proficiency, which I did with only minor hitches. I left the clinic with my morning-after penitential pill, two tubes of spermicidal jelly and my hard-won rubber nestling in its pretty pastel compact. I threw it in the nearest litterbin. If Dominic wanted to have any further truck with me, he would have to come prepared.

8

Renaissance man

Dominic

His cock had taken on a new lease of life. Thanks to Fran. Thanks to his own daredevilry. Yes, he had cast out Impotence in all its forms. Even his Writing Block was chipped; a couple of extra shoves (when he had time) would shatter it completely. A novel was unfurling itself in his head, a novel about a university professor with a wife, a live-in lover, several live-out lovers, and two children, one of whom was mysteriously, wonderfully, and topically black. A little changeling, corporeal signal of the professor's own protean soul. He was Scholar, Poet and Sensualist. . .

But the Book could wait. Dominic's sexual renaissance was long overdue. His renewed priapic gifts made him uncomfortably aware that he had amorous ambitions, ooh-la-la. His marriage was beyond repair. He did not know why. The ruin seemed sudden, but looking back he could see that it was gradual. Now every conversation with Caro could take a nasty turn; the most harmless, even affectionate, remark could transform her into a spitting demoness. 'Don't tell me what to do/say/think! You fuckin' domineering/cunning/egotistical/ arrogant/mean/phoney git!'

Before the Pregnancy, Caro used to sit around all day in a nightdress stained with turmeric and ketchup. Devising ways to inflict pain upon him. Oh, her terrible scornful chuckles, her smell of cigarettes and anger. A close rank sulphurous odour which kept him on his side of the bed. Except once, fatally. One night they got drunk on wine and sentiment. They conjured or remembered desire. Alasdair was the result.

The birth of their son had not so much cemented their marriage as petrified it, both literally and figuratively. Dominic and Caroline were like two appalled immobilized victims of Pompeii. Stuck.

Which was probably why he had protested to Fran last night, as he lay recuperating in her arms: 'But sex does have social and economic consequences, you know!' He was ashamed to overhear that voice of suburban primness emerging from the tangled adulterous sheets. *His* voice.

But she had been expounding her sexual theories. She was against marriage (a tawdry business deal), monogamy (impoverishing, dishonest), family life (battery farms), rigid sex roles (genitalia shouldn't decree destiny).

'Just think how often you check impulses of love in yourself, don't touch or meet someone because you're married, they're married, they're the same sex as you, they're older or younger. . . Oh, just about everyone's out of bounds! We're afraid to touch people emotionally, let alone physically.'

It was hardly polite to challenge her views when he was benefitting so richly from their implementation. But he was irritated. She was surely in a time-warp, a Sixties child, elder sister to one of those doped smilers who used to glide up to strangers in Hyde Park saying 'Wannafuck?'

And what about the consequences? All very well to preach this bighearted love, this hospitable fucking, but where would it lead? Well, everyone knew where it led! Into grimy communal houses where lentil soup was cooked in vats, where kisses, stories, and moral precepts were bestowed without stint by all adults upon a flock of children, who were mostly of obscure lineage. And at the end of each regimented day, you flopped into bed with a fellow outlaw who was big enough not to mind if you cried out the name of another lover in a moment of abandonment.

'Civilisation is based upon restraint,' he instructed.

'What civilisation? Whose restraint?'

'Don't you believe in loyalty?' he said.

'Let me look in your eyes,' she said.

He decided to be discreetly generous with his sperm. Heart, soul, and wallet were another matter. Usually she talked a great deal about herself, a flood of truth, tedious and meticulous: 'Now was it '80 or '81? There was this guy. . . I'll remember his name in a minute. . .' From those confessions, Dominic understood that she was the only child of warring parents. She entered marriage and university almost at the same time and learned disillusion in both. Dominic saw one wedding photograph. A girl in blue silk, her eyes cloudless. A stern bridegroom with a wan bellicose face. He looked like a sick Apache. Their future was all there, in their faces.

'You should have married someone witty,' Dominic told her, getting his belated prescription exactly right. She emerged at twenty-two with a degree and a divorce. Win some, lose some. But since then? Drifting. On a very small raft. Until she succumbed to some passing nigger (Negro. . .black. . .man of colour) and compounded the folly by having the child. Why? Revenge upon her parents, her husband, herself? She had placed herself beyond the peripheries of family life only to gatecrash back in! Did she hate abortion? Maybe she was a Catholic. That would explain her expertise in fellatio. Trained to take the Host in her mouth without any perilous biting impulses. Suddenly he burst into song: 'Fellat-io! Fellat-io!' to the tune of 'Jerusalem'. Yes, she was an Irish Mick. Lax about the fax of life. A romantic with a distaste for contraceptives, uneasy with the application of method to sex. So was he, come to think of it, especially when the burden fell on him! Oh well, *noblesse oblige*, and didn't 'taking precautions' bring back his youth? He wondered how to end this affair? Withdraw slowly, as she had petitioned him in another circumstance. Dominic had been a saint for years, dragging the ball and chain of his virtue everywhere. It was Caroline who had incapacitated him, the bitch! She didn't want him but no one else was allowed to enjoy him. She had punctured his confidence, shrivelled his penis. Well, her power had crumbled!

He would no longer be the incorruptible one communing with angels while his colleagues 'fraternised' with students. Especially those two cognoscenti, Alcock and Pierce, who were often to be espied in secretive pubs sipping shandies with their beauteous charges, often to be overheard discussing their diurnal emissions in the most vulgarian of terms. They pooled their information: there were girls who were 'user-friendly', 'snug-fitting', 'extra-obliging'. There were other girls who were 'frigid', 'hysterical', 'too clever by half', and (darkest of all) 'insatiable'.

The long summer vacation was purgatorial for Alcock and Pierce, their more-than-forty days in the wilderness. They longed for October with its new yield of freshers: reviving prospect! In their parched mouths, the word 'fresher' acquired a nuance of erotic power. What disconcerted and annoyed Dominic was the success of this systematic pair, who seemed so . . . well, homely. Alcock had a horsey laugh and no hair. Pierce had the aroma of the infrequent bather and the surly visage of an Immigration Officer.

While he, Dominic, handsome in a good light and only slightly creased, acted towards his tutees like some discarnate wellwisher. Tending his flowers without ever plucking them. Blowing a gale through the stagnant cranial vaults of people who only wanted a warm breeze. He winced at the memory of a vicious cartoon which Caroline had drawn. Dominic with a suffering Saint Sebastian face attached to the body of a sow, his under-belly dotted with nipples towards which yearned the ravenous mouths of a crowd of piglets with humanoid faces. A human litter. God, it was true! He was milked dry! How easy it would be to obtain some free love. Or at least cutprice.

He could remove those photographs of Caro and Alasdair that sat on his desk like pickets. He thought of all the students who visited him for private tutorials. Shy little sycophants trembling in their trainers. Entering alone into Professor Dalziel's office, the very heart of darkness. Proffering their small underdeveloped tits and their small underdeveloped essays. So eager to please, to concur, to breathe his air, drink at the fount of his wisdom. He could probably sell sachets of his dandruff as keepsakes.

But not to Mona Delahunty, the stout feminist. She was immune both to his real and his bogus charm. There she sat, at the epicentre of his classes, chin on palm, radiating holy disapproval. Some days she was too full of spleen to speak, but one chastising glance from her could sink his self-esteem. On voluble days, she tripped him up at every turn, without hesitation, apology, or deference.

'Hell, I don't concede your point at all!

'Hey, that idea is woefully superficial!

'Can you really not see what the author is getting at?' (intoned with disbelieving pity).

She policed his vocabulary, drawing his mortified attention to the misogynous expressions. A 'tart', she informed him more than once, is a jam-filled edible. A house can't have a wife. An 'old maid' is a woman who has not sold herself to a man. Would he kindly stop defining women as confectionery, birds, flora and fauna, items of landscape, storms and squalls, wombs and vaginas? Was his knowledge of women writers *really* confined to Virginia, Charlotte and Jane?

Mona's essays were rare and manic: a diatribe accusing Ted Hughes of murdering Sylvia Plath. A brilliant two-page parody in blank verse of *Paradise Lost*. Mona didn't want a degree from this contemptible institution. She would not be judged by her inferiors. A determined under-achiever. Proof of sincerity and perhaps even of ability. Why did she keep attending classes, then? Did she have a mission, Queen Canute standing before a polluted ocean? Dominic suspected that she came to persecute him. Her aim was unilateral disarmament: his. Other students of the female persuasion in that group had grown combustible under her influence. They had stopped smiling. God, it was sinister when women didn't smile.

Mona had organised a cabal against him. Well, not just against him. Against Male Power. Men. (Three legs bad, two legs good!) Last term the Wimmin protested to the Faculty about course content (womyn's achievements not reflected). They submitted duplicated essays to several different teachers to expose their divergent and biassed marking. They were in the process of compiling a hefty dossier on sexual harassment, in which 'names would be named'. (Dominic hastily dropped Darling, Love, Dear, and Sweetheart from his arsenal.) They demanded and got free self-defence classes. It was rumoured that they were being trained to kill a man in thirty seconds flat! Dominic's office was near their gym. Every day he had to walk past that place of shrieks, and he could well believe it.

He guarded his patriarchal tongue. 'Mankind' became 'humanity'. 'He' became (inelegantly) 'he or she'. He studded his talks (he didn't dare call them 'lectures' any more) with quotes from such diverse women authors as De Beauvoir, Anna Wickham, H.. D.

It cut no ice. His hegemony went on collapsing. It was so unfair. After all, Dominic was a Feminist. He loved women. He was in favour of foreplay, vibrators, women drivers, and Virago paperbacks! Once he had even looked in on the Men's Group, determined to do everything he could to launder his consciousness. He had sat for hours on a hard chair surrounded by pale men vying with each other in non-assertion. Men grizzling about their inability either to have or exhibit feeling, he wasn't sure which. One embittered member was so jealous of women's 'emotional privileges'. He wanted the right to cry! He managed to give birth to one little teardrop, to murmurs of envy and encouragement. Well, Dominic's feelings were titanic, his weepings healthily frequent! O Mona! How she humiliated him with her jibes and scoldings. Made him dance in front of her. A twisted faltering little dance of shame and secret euphoria. Her glare sent a thousand volts of desire through him. He loved her. She was the one.

He scanned classic fiction for clues on means of seduction in such a hard case. No use. Phantom lovers lying together between typed sheets had it easy. Their passions always weighed the same. They inflamed each other with eloquent looks and twitches, a muted but unmistakable semaphore.

In reality, mating rituals were brutal, grosser, he thought. Bald statements of lust, grab and stab. Impossible! Mona would probably (definitely) pulverise him before he could whip out his compliment. In one recurrent fantasy, she came meltingly to him, doe-eyed and sweet. Joyfully he yielded to her. His other fantasies were rapacious, sometimes vengeful. She was sprawled across his desk (scene of so much heavy labour!) Naked apart from her iridescent socks. Impaled on his joystick. Writhing beneath her merciless benefactor in an ecstasy of subjection.

But how to introduce her to the Golden Bough? Never ever ever, he thought.

The house was empty all afternoon. Dominic locked himself in the bathroom with a razor. He began cautiously, tremulously. There. He had started; he must go all the way. Soon his Ken Livingstone moustache was no more. Success! Dominic admired his renovated image. A bare upper lip made him look so vulnerable. In the bathroom cabinet he found some skin lotions and a packet of henna, that smelled like dried cowdung. Might as well, he thought. He mixed and applied the muddy paste to his hair. While it dried he sat humming on the toilet, waiting for enhancement.

He *would* have Mona. He deserved her. He should have anyone he wanted. Women and girls — and youths. Why not? Robin Freeman. Mona and Robin, terrorist twins, his Scylla and Charydbis. Ah, Robin, the scornful, myopic Rimbaud. Dominic imagined removing the boy's glasses. . . The phone rang. Shrilly, on and on. . . Dominic did not hear.

He was listening to the oncoming traffic of his lovers.

9

Sleepless Nights

Fran

The more I made love with Dominic, the more I thought about Caroline. She was restless, full of a grim sullen vigour which made her pace the floor, change her clothes several times a day, drive off in the car 'nowhere in particular'. She was always trying on new clothes, new lovers, new identities both on and off stage. What are you searching for? I wondered. Fleeing from? Sometimes she looked like a prisoner fresh out of jail, standing blinking on the pavement.

My own energies dwindled as hers increased. I seemed to be perpetually tired, wearied by the ceaseless demands of the babies, the battle with the crumbs and dust, the scouring of the burnt pans. It took the edge off my guilt. It took away the future.

In Caroline's presence, Dominic treated me with abstract good will, curbing his usual gallantry. Towards her, he was offhand and imperturbable. Our sexual scenes were more talkative than torrid, growing comfortably out of our cosy dialogues in his study. He started off wistfully, tenderly, quizzing me with things like: 'Would you marry me if I were free?' Later he would mutter (to himself? to me?) incoherent phrases, dark drifting utterances: 'Women aren't. . . Why this?. . . Nothing can . . . You . . . Never. . .'

Then would follow his spiritual crisis. Much activity of the tear ducts. He lined up his regrets: failed childhood, failed marriage, meaningless accomplishments, his hiding away, polishing his footnotes in a University Ivory Tower. I was another item of remorse. But he wasn't an ordinary man, he needed, deserved some violent emotion, didn't he? He would glance at his watch and decide that we must return to 'reality'. He would become fatherly, protective. 'What are you doing here with me? Do you hate me? Live, live to the hilt, do you hear? Promise?'

I cultivated irony. I started to counter his questions about my theoretical willingness to marry him with some astringent queries of my own: 'Would you bother with this affair, if I lived a mile away? Or even half a mile?' I told myself he was just an attractive fraud full of winsome melancholy. I amassed evidence against him. No use. I had fallen in love. Inadvertently. Inch by inch. A black shockwave of jealousy every time he spoke fondly to Caroline, every time he looked with pleasure at something not-me: a book, a cake, the sky. It got worse. Sleepless nights. Standing barefoot at my bedroom door, listening.

Caroline and Dominic. Their marriage seemed threadbare, worn down with testy tedious rows. He didn't seem to know about her hardworking infidelities. Or perhaps. . .? What was between them? What violent connection? Hatred? Dependence? Some sexual secret?

I remembered my own parents marooned together, sexless, bickering, lonely, eyes fixed on each other. The sickening exclusive power of marriage with its rings and photos, its rights and atrocities!

Dominic

It was after nine when he brought her a cup of coffee. Freshly brewed and strong. A large dose of caffeine to spring her finally out of bed. She sipped it carefully while he watched her in a solicitous exacting way as if she were taking medicine.

'You don't get up early any more, Fran,' he chided her gently. It was difficult being both employer and lover, he realised. He understood now why his mother had always insisted on a kind of genteel apartheid from the cleaners who used to remove the family dirt. Still, Fran did look fetching with her hair all rumpled and a baby in the crook of each arm! A wanton Madonna.

She sighed. 'I get up at bloody dawn! You think those babies don't cry in the morning, don't you? Know why? Because as soon as they start roaring, I'm there! And sometimes I'm so tired I just have to cart them back to bed with me in the hope that I can doze off again!'

'You could smother them,' he opined, so mildly it sounded more like a suggestion than a rebuke.

'No! I sleep sitting up when they're here.'

'Like the Elephant Man?'

'Oughtn't you to bring Caroline some coffee?'

'She's out,' he leered.

'Where?'

'Jogging. In her primrose jump suit and her alluring little pink ankle socks. . . Jesus, I'm cold. Let me in,' he said, lifting the duvet so that he could slide in beside her. Oh, *slide*! he thought. *In*!

'Get out!' She was appalled.

'Aw, come on! I'm not going to . . . take liberties with your person!'

'Caroline. . .'

'I've told Caroline about us,' he said with casual cruelty.

'Liar!'

'No, I'm not.'

'Oh, God! What did you say to her? Dominic!'

'Well, she informed me that she would be home late tonight again. So, naturally, I said: "That's fine. It'll give me and Fran more time to make love." And she just laughed. You see, I always tell her the truth and she never believes me. It's quite a good system.'

'I hate you both!'

He tweaked her left breast. 'That's rather extreme of you.'

'I wish we'd never started this!'

'We?' he reminded her.

'I've been reading this report by a Kenyan woman about the miseries of putting up with a co-wife. The way the new wife, the queen she calls her, eclipses the old one, who's ignored and maltreated and made to sleep on the floor. A co-wife, that's what I am! A betrayer of other women!'

'You're very influenced by what you read, aren't you? Must get you *The 120 Days of Sodom*.

'Why 120 days?'

'What?'

'It's almost exactly a third of a year. There must be some significance? O Dominic, stop touching me!'

'You like it.'

'Not in daylight. Not in the presence of. . . Not with Caroline probably racing down the street this minute.'

'Guilt and jealousy and risk are the whole point of adultery!'

'Ah, that's what I thought!' She flashed him a very wifely look. A look of aggressive vindicated cynicism. 'Caroline isn't an obstacle to our relationship! She's the impetus.'

'For you, perhaps?' he asked.

'What do you mean?'

'It's chilly in here. I shall seek warmth elsewhere. Terry Wogan show or something.'

Ten minutes later he returned. It was tactically wrong, it was craven, but he could not resist Fran when she was upbraiding him. She was half-dressed now in a long red shirt that covered her hips but revealed a few tantalising curls of her muff.

'Caroline's indispensable to you!' she said, and he knew that he was interrupting a scolding that had gone on in his absence.

'She's what enables you to call your sluggishness heroism! "My wife, my son": you treat them like protective talismans! It's not that you're too caring to leave her. You haven't the guts! You haven't the. . . the love! Why would you leave one woman you don't love for another woman you don't love!'

The tragic potential of her tirade was undermined by the irreverent little beard that kept displaying itself as she moved. Oh, the farce of the human body! What a fantastic shirt, though! he thought. Deep warm red. Scarlet. *Scarlet*!

'I'm glad you think it's funny!'

He advanced on her. 'God, you're beautiful!' he throbbed.

'On your bike! On your bloody tandem!'

'I didn't realize you wanted me to leave Caroline.'

'I don't! What do you take me for?'

'Ah!'

Pink dots appeared on her cheeks; her ice blue stare faltered. His penis swelled with generosity and forgiveness.

'Fran,' he said firmly and she rushed weeping into his grip.

One of the babies made a sound like laughter.

10

A Journey

Caroline   *Greenham*

'Can't find that other flask,' Fran was complaining as Caroline entered the house by the kitchen door.

'Oh, you're back. Just in time, too,' Dominic said. He was dressed in several layers of cladding: one light and one heavy sweater, warm trousers, jacket and overcoat, scarf, wellies, and, to crown the ensemble, a suede and sheepskin deerstalker. Caroline could tell that he was enormously proud of the costume. A similarly well-padded Fran was now searching for sandwich boxes.

'What are you pair up to? Eloping? Are you really serious about that hat?'

'We're off to Greenham,' Fran said briskly. 'There's been a call. The Cruise convoy has been sighted on Salisbury Plain. It's on its way back. Supporters are needed up there to protest and raise the alarm.'

'I'm coming with you,' Caroline announced to her own surprise.

Exchange of constrained looks.

'You?'

'Yes, me!' she insisted with a mixture of determination and appeal.

'I didn't know you were anti-Cruise,' Fran said.

'Never asked, did you?'

'The babies, Caro,' Dominic spoke. 'Someone has to stay behind to look after the babies.'

'Bring them with us.'

'No! I am not pelting round the countryside at night with two infant passengers! This is not a picnic outing, you know!'

'You could have fooled me!' she eyed the mound of sandwiches and peanut bags.

Fran spoke decisively. 'Dominic, why don't you stay here and look after the children, while Caroline and I go?'

'But I've gotten myself ready!' he wailed.

'Aw, all dressed up and nowhere to go. Shame, isn't it, Fran?'

A strange quiet jubilation filled the air between the two women. The

74

sudden accidental shift in alliances made everything fresh and pleasurably alarming. What had triggered it?

'You're ganging up on me! I'm not to be allowed to inflict my contaminatory male presence. Mustn't trespass into the domain of the Goddess. That's it, isn't it?' They smirked but would not answer. He turned to practical objections.

'You've never driven to Newbury, Caro. Neither has Fran. You'll get lost.'

'It's not exactly uncharted territory! And we do have a map.'

'What if you get arrested? You could get hurt, you know.'

'Your presence wouldn't stop that from happening.'

'But at least I would know. I could do something. God, I'll be so worried about you! No, I'm not having it. If I don't go, no one goes!'

'Oh yes we are!' Caroline and Fran chorused, breaking into laughter at Dominic's face which looked so aggrieved and fatuously important beneath the ridiculous hat.

'Right!' he said. 'So be it! I'm overruled. You can go off and be the twin scourge of the combined American and British militia or whatever naive Supergirl notions you want to indulge! And I,' he concluded grandly, 'shall act as babysitter!'

'They also serve who only stand and wait,' Caroline quipped, but Fran turned to him in a hot fury: 'Sometimes I hate you, Dominic!'

'How very passionate!' He cleared his throat. 'Well, mustn't detain you. The world is urgently waiting for your message of love and peace!'

He marched out, leaving both women staring at the space he had occupied, reluctant to face each other.

Fran spoke first: 'Shouldn't have said that! But just think of most women's lives! Waiting. Worrying. Working in all kinds of behind-the-scenes ways. . . And he makes such a song and dance over one miserable evening!'

'You don't have to tell me! Look, let's make our escape before he composes any more stinging remarks! Just give me a minute to get into some jeans.'

'And sensible shoes.'

'I know. I know. I bags the driving. You can bring us back.'

They worked out the route in the car. It was pitch dark as they progressed slowly through the traffic of West London. Caroline relaxed when they reached the motorway and started making headway towards Reading.

'It won't take long,' she said.

'Why did you come?' Fran asked, without looking at her.

'Same reasons as you, I expect. Well, if you really want to know. . . First because you didn't want me to, and then because you did.'

They laughed, dispelling the residue of tension between them.

'And why did you suddenly ditch Dominic?'

'I suppose I'm tired of. . . I don't know. . . of being under his jurisdiction.'

'Good for you.'

'I dare say he'll sulk for at least a week after this!'

'He's much too crafty for that.'

'What do you mean?'

'You'll find out.'

Fran spoke of her first visit to the Common just six weeks after Emily's birth. It was the major demonstration on 12 December 1982, when women decorated the whole nine miles of the perimeter fence with symbols and objects of value. There were babies' clothes, toys, family photographs, flowers, woven webs.

'All those personal and homely things in that cold menacing place. As if a huge band of women exiled to Saturn had made a retrospective exhibition of their earthly souvenirs. Someone tied a hank of human hair, black glossy hair, to the fence, and I wanted to ask her if it was her lover's, her child's? Was the person alive or dead? But I couldn't speak to her. That hair looked so holy in that place. Oh, that sounds daft. . .'

'No! Go on.'

'There was another woman there who put up pictures of three generations of men in her family who had been killed or maimed in wars. God, the toll on one family of even conventional war! I studied the photographs. Men in uniforms. They all looked really likeable and unintimidating. And I realised that they couldn't be so different from the soldiers and policemen all around us!'

'Apart from the degree of rigor mortis!'

'That's arguable!'

They laughed.

Fran went on seriously: 'What I mean is, going there made me less scared of police and soldiers. Not that they're not frightening. They are. But in Belfast, they were just . . . hurting machines. My heart skipped a beat every time I saw a uniform. Though it was worse when you didn't see them. I mean, in front of every police station over there they have a sentry box. All you can see is an eye watching you from a peephole and a rifle butt sticking through a narrow slit. Sometimes the

76

soldiers in there mutter things at women passing by. Obscenities, threats of rape, the usual. And you tell yourself that it's just some spotty little sadist bored out of his skull. But it's terrifying, anyway. That sentry box all round him like a giant rapist's hood . . . But at Greenham, that day, my fear started to be outweighed by a whole new mixture of feelings, pity and contempt and hope.'

'You've never talked this way before,' Caroline said.

'We stopped talking, didn't we?'

'Well, I know I placed you in an invidious position by talking about my affairs. I suppose you thought I was out to hurt Dominic.'

'I had no right to condemn you.'

' "Condemn!" Is that what you did? As strong as that?'

'I thought you were trying to humiliate Dominic by telling me. I felt used! I thought you were rubbing my nose in your unhappiness.' Her face was bright crimson. 'Please don't talk about it! We'd better find a loo before we get to the base.'

Caroline agreed. 'We should bring something for the women as well.'

'Brandy?'

'Yes, and what about some food?'

'Non-perishable is best.'

'How appropriate,' Caroline laughed.

They stopped at a pub to buy the goods and use the toilet. Back on the road, they grew silent as they neared the camp, each busy with her own inner soliloquy. The road outside the Orange gate was lined with protestors' cars.

'What's happening?' Fran asked a man parked next to them.

'Nothing yet. The women think it'll show up before dawn. Where have you come from?'

'London.'

'I'm from Oxford, but I've been trailing all over Salisbury Plain looking for the damn convoy. Wild goose chase.'

Fran and Caroline milled among the bystanders. The information was scant and conflicting. People offered drinks or nibbles: the camaraderie of shared inadequacy.

'Let's go over,' Caroline suggested.

They wandered towards a group of women seated on logs around a camp fire.

'My God,' Caroline whispered as she took in the desolation of the camp. Mud everywhere. Impossibly low and frail-looking polythene

77

dwellings: the famous 'benders' made by draping plastic sheets over pliant boughs pegged into the mud. She saw a new vellum writing pad lying on the ground, its sheets dimpled and curled from the dampness. The sight of it touched her absurdly.

'How could anyone sleep in those things?' Caroline said, pointing to the fragile shelters.

'I think mostly the women don't sleep. Especially at this gate. It's very noisy.'

In silence a woman offered them two bits of cardboard to sit on. It was the only acknowledgement of their presence. Caroline felt awkwardly self-conscious. Were they being gently snubbed? Two 'soft' part-time heroines? But gradually she realised that it was a matter of instant acceptance, and that it was the first time she had entered a strange group without the sense of parading on a catwalk.

Here were punks and pensioners conversing in the friendliest ease.

Caroline started to chat with an elderly woman wrapped in a blanket. Her eyes streamed constantly from the cold. She was a retired nurse, she said. She was there for the sake of her children and grandchildren. She showed Caroline her plastic folder full of clippings about the dangers of radiation, evidence that even low levels are more hazardous than previously thought. Conservative estimates of deaths from cancer caused by the A Bomb tests in the fifties: between 29,000 and 72,000. Genetic effects: 168,000. Testicular cancer greatly on the increase in men born during that period. Caroline felt sick. 'I wonder if all those joggers and vitamin freaks know about this?'

'You can spread this knowledge. People must be warned.'

Suddenly a fire engine appeared, lights flashing. Men jumped down and started extinguishing the women's fires.

'For God's sake! How spiteful and petty can they get?' The woman shrugged. Her eyes were full of a kind of wishless stoicism.

'We'll light it again, dear. After they've gone.' It grew later and colder and darker. Caroline stood up stiffly and went to find Fran, who was peering through the fence at the silos.

'It's so ghostly here. As if it had already been the site of a mass extermination.'

'Why don't you come over and talk.'

'I don't want to.'

'Why?'

'I'm ashamed to talk to those women. They're enduring so much. And people like me turn up in emergencies bearing little guilt offerings.'

'Fran, let's drive round to the main gate.'

'Why?'

'I overheard someone say that's where it'll come in. They'll avoid this gate because things are too well prepared here with that barricade of cars.'

At the main gate Caroline stood on the roadside scanning the distant traffic. Every large extra-luminous pair of headlamps made her anxious, but they all belonged to ordinary lorries. A police car moved along the road, stopping and starting. An officer inside was ostentatiously noting down the protestors' number plates.

'Maybe it won't come at all,' Fran said. 'They'll wait until the crowd has dispersed.'

But then a woman shouted from a car window that the convoy was coming; it was only about ten minutes away. Caroline and Fran went to lie down in the road with other women.

Suddenly police were everywhere, pouring out of their white vans. They appeared as though by magic, transforming the area into something like a Chinese township, full of identically clad citizens.

'Aren't you ashamed?' a woman yelled at them. 'You're *our* police! This is *our* land. The British people did not vote for these missiles!'

She screamed as she was dragged along the ground. Caroline saw the head of the convoy. A huge vehicle with motorcycle outriders. 'O Christ,' she thought. 'What if the driver goes berserk and . . .?' Images of death from her childhood flickered swiftly through her mind. Sydney Carton walking to the scaffold in Darnay's stead. A moth's wing melting in candleflame. A dead owl in the garden. 'Don't touch. There'll be fleas,' her mother had said. She had a sudden vision of her mother listening to a Sibelius concert on the radio, her face rapt. 'She loved music. She really loved it,' Caroline realised for the first time. 'O Mum, Mum . . .'

The eyes of the woman beside her were closed in nausea or prayer. She turned and found herself looking straight at Fran. They stared at each other in deep speechless connection until they were dragged away and herded into one of the vans. Some women began to sing:

'Whose side are you on? Are you on the side of Suicide? Are you on the side of Genocide? Whose side are you on?' It took the police only minutes to clear the road. The fifty foot carrier lurched forward and promptly broke down. It *broke down*! Momentary disbelief on both sides. Jeers and slow handclaps while flustered mechanics began to fix it.

When the convoy was 'safely' inside the base, everybody was released without charge. Caroline's nerves were frayed. Fran started to remove the layers of clay from her boots.

'Oh, do wait until it dries!' Caroline snapped at her.

'Let's have some of that coffee and food we brought.' The snack revived them and they prepared to drive home.

'It's my turn to drive,' Fran said. 'We've got in the wrong sides.'

'Oh, shit.'

They changed seats.

'Fran, I don't want to go home yet.'

'I can't wait to get away from here!'

'I know! I mean, I want to go to Stonehenge. All that talk about Salisbury Plain has given me the notion.'

'It's miles away!'

'It's not that far. We can do a round trip. Back to London by Andover.'

'What about Dominic?'

'That's all right. He doesn't go in till later on Thursdays.'

'But he'll be worried.'

'Will he? You can ring him if you like.'

Still she hesitated.

'Ever seen Stonehenge? At dawn?' Caroline said slyly.

'Oh, Caroline, it won't work.'

'What won't work?'

'You know. Visiting another centre of power. A different kind of power.'

'It's a feeling I have, that we shouldn't drive out here just to be defeated and slink back home.'

'What will the campers do to alleviate their sense of defeat?'

'They're still there. That's their triumph.'

'OK, we'll go to bloody Stonehenge. You'd better guide me well, though!'

On the way, Fran was quiet, concentrating on driving.

'Can't get that song out of my head,' Caroline said. 'Su-i-cide. Gen-o-cide . . . When I was a child, there was this man who worked for my dad. He told me about how animals are killed in the abattoir. It upset me so much and I kept questioning my mother about it. She swore that the animals had no inkling of what was going to happen to them. No foreboding. Not in the trucks, not in the pens, not in the anteroom. But I didn't believe her. I was sure that some animals must

80

know. I imagined them all stricken and wide-eyed. Crying in their particular ways: a whole cacophony of bleats and snuffles and lowing. I thought that some of them could surely smell the blood before they reached the slaughterhouse. And that's the difference between those women and everybody else. They can smell the blood.'

It was sunrise when they reached Stonehenge. They stopped some way off at first to watch the plinths against the glowing sky. Then they approached the monument on foot and climbed over the fence. They leaned against one of the stones.

'There's so much of the world I haven't seen,' Fran said.

Caroline looked at her with curiosity. 'What do you want to do with yourself?' she said.

'Don't know. I can't camp out in your house forever.'

'You're very welcome,' Caroline said coolly.

'Oh, I don't mean . . . It's just that I feel like a bystander in life.'

'Will you look for work?'

'Work!' Fran said scornfully.

'*Meaningful* work,' Caroline said in mock solemn tones.

'I hate that word. "Meaningful" work, "meaningful" relationships, "meaningful" silences. Caroline, do you love Dominic?'

She laughed. 'I'm feeling benign towards everyone just now, even my husband!'

'That's not exactly an ardent declaration.'

'O Fran, you know what marriage is like,' she said. 'Days and days of indifference or low-pitched spite, and then suddenly he says something or looks a certain way that stabs your memory and there's a revival of feeling, a sweet painful revival . . . What's wrong? Maybe I shouldn't have talked about marriage.'

'You deserve better than that!' Fran burst out, and Caroline rushed to kiss her cold cheek and press her face into her hair that smelt of oranges and woodsmoke. It was the first time she had ever kissed a woman out of affection rather than protocol.

11

Skin

Caroline isn't an obstacle to our relationship. She's the impetus!'
  'For you, perhaps?'
  Could it be . . .? I reflected on it for days until everything became
shaming and obvious. I had systematically and savagely discarded the
privileges and comforts of my parents' home only to find myself in a
similar treacherous haven! Once again living in anxious covetous
speculation about the relationship between a couple. My affair with
Dominic was a classic cliché. I was punishing Mummy. I was comfort-
ing Daddy because Mummy didn't love him. It explained my love-hate
for Caroline. She had none of my mother's vicious splendour, her
monstrous vanity and loneliness. And yet there were resemblances.
Caroline was domineering, tempestuous, theatrical. There was something lost about her. She *glittered*. What a joke! I was a hater of Freud
and yet trapped in a textbook Electra complex. Electra. Elect. I could
always elect to leave. Couldn't I?

One day I was wheeling the children down to the local park,
thankful to get away from the domestic pressure chamber. A girl
darted alonside me. Frowning white face, pale sandy eyelashes.
She was carrying a child's beach bucket, which she rattled at
me.
  'Give something to help the orphans, Missus?'
  'I don't think you're authorized to collect for them, are you?'
  'Just ten pee,' she wheedled.
  I was forced to look at her. She seemed weak and cunning, like an
unhealthy animal.
  'Go on, for my bus fare, Missus.'
  'Please go away.'
  'Them babies yours, Missus?'
  'Yes, they are.'
  'I'm hungry,' she said, suddenly childlike.

I dug into my pockets, placed some coins in her outstretched unsurprised hand.

'Nigger-lover,' she whispered before scurrying off. My heart was banging.

'I can't be affected by a little bitch like that,' I told myself. It wasn't true.

'Hypersensitive,' Dominic would say. 'Too thin-skinned,' Caroline would say.

Thin skin. Black skin.

I looked at Emily asleep in the pram. What am I going to do?, I asked her silently.

I began to steer clear of Dominic and Caroline, retreating to my own room after putting the babies to bed. Locking my door.

I borrowed books from Dominic's study, stacks of documentary-style expositions of current affairs. I skimmed over the texts of these books and concentrated on the photographs. Women in the Transkei staring at the camera. Blaming no one. Separated from their men. Their children starving.

Ethiopia. A lone woman with a skeletal baby on her back stooping over a puddle of dirty water. Her agonized expression as she cups the water in her hands and brings it towards her mouth.

Is she still alive? Is she dead?

Maimed and bleeding bodies in the Lebanon, Iraq, Ireland. The blood always black and still in these pictures, not the way I remembered it on Irish streets, bright, glistening, spreading.

Dying made intimate yet distant, imaginary.

Namibian workers outside the British-owned Rossing mine. Emaciated and hollow-eyed. They die quickly from handling the uranium which yields the plutonium which is needed for the manufacture of the nuclear weapons which are needed to protect us from the nuclear weapons which . . .

The moment of extinction or loss was a firm favourite with these cameramen, these chroniclers of death. El Salvador. A woman crying out in rage and disbelief, her mouth an angry black hole. A man kneeling . . . I stared until he turned into a mass of black and white grainy dots. But it was a man kneeling beside his own grave. A gun pressed against his temple. Eyes screwed tight. His final moment, frozen, permanent. I was joining in an execution. The helpless witness. The accomplice. I understood the paralysing effect of such pictures.

83

They revealed simultaneously the guilt and powerlessness of the onlooker. They shocked me into their own stasis. 'Death' they whispered. 'Death is all around you, it's everywhere! The human condition . . . nobody's fault . . . give in . . . give up . . . bow to the inevitable . . . line up quietly outside the crematorium . . .'

'No,' I thought. 'No. I say *No*.'

12

Out

Dominic

It's crazy! Absolutely barmy! How will you manage? What will you do with Emily?'

'I've already explained. I'm going to share a house in Belsize Park with four women. Two of them have children also. We'll take it in turns going to Greenham. One week on the protest, one week looking after the children.'

Dominic was silent for a few minutes. 'You would have come out of that hospital to no one and nothing if it hadn't been for us,' he complained, but she said nothing, just kept staring into her empty glass. 'And now you think you can just up and leave! . . . My son has grown attached to you, you know! We all have . . .'.

'Oh, don't remind me!'

'So that's it! Look, Fran, don't be childish. There's no call for you to go off and do penance on some "blasted heath" just because we got slightly overfriendly . . . Caro doesn't know about it . . . Anyway, we're grown-up people. We're not into jealousy and all that *crime passionel* stuff!'

'O Dominic, don't be so . . . so self-important. OK, I don't feel great about what happened . . . about what we did, deceiving Caroline, but that's not why . . . I'm not going to Greenham to purify myself! It's more to do with Emily than with you. I have a stake in the future now. I would like there to *be* a future. And I want to do something useful. There must be more to life than this . . . surrogate wifehood!'

'You see, it is that! You're just a provincial puritan seeking chastisement. Know what's wrong with you? I think you really miss all that Belfast blood 'n' guts, all those marches and rallies and police brutalities. You have a nostalgia for confrontation. Queen-sized Joan of Arc complex, that's you!'

His raised voice seemed to have created a pocket of silence around them. He realised that people were openly listening, their eyes swivelling from one protagonist to the other as they tried to pick the victor.

'Everything you say is probably true.'

'Right!'

'But it doesn't matter.'

'What do you mean, it doesn't matter?' he hissed.

'It doesn't matter why I go, only *whether* I go. I won't discuss it any more. It's none of your business. Why is it that no one ever challenges people about why they *don't* go? Conformity and obedience are never taken to task even when they might lead to . . . People would rather risk being incinerated than arrested! What's so sane about that?'

'O God, look who's coming!'

Two acquaintances were approaching with grins and tankards.

'Do you know them?'

'Yes. Bloody Nigel and bloody Priscilla. I work with him, or rather I work against him. Bloody reactionary Leavisite!'

'Hello there, Dalziel!' Nigel said with sneering affability. 'Mind if we join you?' He ogled Fran. 'And who's this, then? One of your extramurals, I suppose?'

'Fran is a friend.'

'I look after Dominic's son.' The replies were simultaneous and icy.

'Say that again!' he requested sweetly to Fran.

'What? I look after Dominic's son.'

'She's a wee colleen! And what part o' the Emerald Isle d'ye come from?'

'North-east. And what part of Albion do you and your wench come from?'

Nigel laughed doggedly. 'Ah, a spitfire. You have your hands full there, Dalziel!'

Dominic observed anxiously the trio's complicated crisscross of glares and spread his hands in a plea for good will and harmony.

'Priscilla, can I get you something?' he said.

'No thanks.'

'Fran? . . . Another orange juice?'

'I'd like champagne this time,' she said coldly.

'Why? You hate champagne!'

'Get the girl some champers, you can afford it!' Nigel jeered.

When Dominic came back with the drinks, Nigel had abandoned his suggestive tone and was questioning Fran with exaggerated courtesy.

'Oh, from Belfast! And how long have you been in London?'

'Five years.'

'Ever want to go back up there?'

'No.'

'Don't blame you. All those nutters. What are they fighting for, eh?'

'It's in their blood,' Priscilla pronounced.

'Beyond all reason. Totally stupid,' Nigel said.

'Do you always call things stupid if you don't understand them?' Fran said softly.

Nigel's voice wavered. 'Perhaps you would care to enlighten me?'

'I don't have that much time.'

'But I would so much value your elucidation.'

'The homegrown nutters in Ulster are only part of the problem.'

'Here we go!' said Priscilla triumphantly.

Dominic intervened. 'Fran . . .'

'Let me speak, Dominic! I'm tired of this wilful English ignorance, all this headshaking complicity! You'd think we had Greek soldiers patrolling the streets up there!'

Dominic stood up. 'Would you excuse us, please, Nigel? Priscilla? I'm afraid we were in the middle of discussing a rather crucial matter. We had hoped to be private.'

Nigel leered. 'Of course.'

'I mean, Fran has decided to join the protest at Greenham.'

'Dominic! It's none of their business!'

Priscilla banged her glass down on the table. 'In fact, it's none of *your* business! What has Britain's defence policy to do with you? Don't shush me, Dominic! I know these loud-mouthed Irish. Swallowing our taxes, coming over here in droves to take our jobs and vote in our elections, planting their bombs and then whining about the Prevention of Terrorism Act. Oh yes, we should make it easier for them to murder us! Listen to her, an IRA supporter telling us we should disarm! That's a laugh! When have the Irish ever been interested in Britain's welfare?'

Fran's lips were retracted in a kind of smile. 'Do you know the words of "God Save the Queen", Priscilla? I do. Every word of every stanza. I know that to someone of your education we Irish are just one big homogeneous bunch of demented Paddies, but in the north-east corner of Ireland where I come from, we're British citizens. Some are reluctant and some are enthusiastic about it. I was brought up to exult in being an honorary Brit. It didn't work in my case, and meeting people like you confirms the disenchantment! You see, when I was growing up, it shocked me to realise that some of my compatriots saw me and my kind as oppressors and usurpers and with good reason. I felt

I had no right to be there. I didn't belong. And now you're telling me I have no right to be here. Well, you're wrong. I can't be dispossessed any more.'

'No? I'm sure you're more interested in being possessed. By any man that crosses the road.'

'Oh, is that what's bothering you, Priscilla? There's really no need to be jealous.'

'Don't kid yourself! My Nigel wouldn't have you if you paid him.'

'Always ready to consider a reasonable offer!' Nigel joked. 'Ladies, dear ladies, this is getting a bit heav-ee!'

But Fran was already walking proudly towards the door. Dominic followed her with maximum audience attention. In the street she marched ahead of him.

'Fran, Fran!'

'Leave me alone.'

'Where are you going? Aren't you coming home in the car?'

'Home?' She started to cry and he embraced her.

'Hey, take it easy. That was a fine demonstration of sisterhood and pacifism,' he cajoled her gently.

'All women are not my friends.'

'Clearly.'

They laughed.

'Fran, you don't have to take on the whole world. Or save it either.'

'It's *my* world. And there are no frontiers any more. The Bomb has done away with frontiers.'

'Maybe. But I still see plenty of barricades around you.'

He felt her relax and lean against him. 'I'm still going, Dominic.'

'A girl's gotta do what a girl's gotta do.'

'I'm a woman, Dominic,' she said quietly.

'I know, remember? Fran, don't rush into leaving. Think it over for a while.'

She'll stay, he thought.

13

Sword

(handwritten: Dominic / Words → Fran)

Dominic came home one day to find a stranger in the house.

'Who are you?'

'Ginny! You remember me! I used to do a lot of babysitting.'

He dashed upstairs to Fran's room. She wouldn't go without warning? She wasn't so mean?

She had taken everything except books, tapes, papers, a cassette-player. The tapes were unlabelled. Idly, Dominic inserted one into the machine. Nothing. 'Must be blank,' he decided and was moving to switch it off when a voice, low but fierce as the elements, started to speak.

'Don't you look at me no squinty-eyed way, girl! I'm sick of it, yeah! Had me my fill. Don't want no harassment offa you. Enough torment, girl, enough hassle without you adding no aggravation. Know who you put me in mind of? My English teacher, yeah! Miss Sealy, only she ain't no Miss, she call herself Mizz Sealy, like you're supposed to wonder do she have a man or do she not. Well, she have not! Wanta bet on it? Tightass like you. Too stuck up to have no manfriend. Yeah, that's the way she looks at me too. Like I'm some kinda bad stink. Police do it too. Can't even walk down my own street without police coming at me with their meanmouth questions. And me keeping my eyes skint case they put their dope on me. Got nobody looking out for me. Paddling my own canoe. Got to handle yourself with pride. Only don't talk about it. Guys who talk pride all the time got none. Like guys who talk money. My friend was like that. He's dead now. Throat cut. Did it to himself, police said. Suicide, they said! I'll tell you what's suicide. Suicide is coming to this pissing country in the first place. Slow way of dying far from home. Having kiddies what is called Black Britons. No such thing as a Black Briton! No such thing as a pig with wings. Maybe there be pigs what think they got wings, but aren't no pigs up in the sky!

Suicide is them bad looks and bad words going into you, driving into you, all the time till you believe you're nothing but shit and turn your

(handwritten right margin: Cornelius / story of)

89

own hand against yourself! See, Britain not my home! Jamaica not my home! No place my home! . . .

Had me a white girl, you know. Yeah. A beauty, not no white trash. Looked a bit like you, only with style, know what I mean?

Fran's voice: 'Oh, a minute ago I looked like Miss Sealy.'

'Whites all look the same to me. Anyway, Sealy couldn't stand the sight of me with Karen. Her eyes pop out of her head and she goes red with covetousness and spite, girl, like I done something real bad but real clever too. And so she mouths about it to all her colleague cunts and they start leering and insinuating and giving Karen a hard time. It's like all of a sudden my Karen is dirt. But sexy, yeah, so sexy but right outa reach, because no white dick is every gonna do her no good now. Cos black man delivers a supreme fuck, that's what they believe, that's what they're scared of. I'm not saying they're wrong. So things go from bad to worse, Karen and me get no peace. Last straw comes when Smithwaite, that's the Geography teacher-cunt, he calls Karen a name in front of the whole class. He calls her a 'groundsheet for the darkies'. Makes her cry. She's not used to it like me. I tell her don't fret cos I will break his face and she says no, it only makes me look a savage the way he says. And she drops me a couple days later. Says that not the reason, but what other reason can there be, girl?

Gonna make them pay. Smithwaite. Spread that fat nose all over his face. Sealy. Gonna fuck her till them sneaky eyes roll back in her head. "Vengeance is mine," says the Lord. The time be coming, yeah, the time be near at hand . . .'

Dominic's hand shook as he switched off the machine. So this was Emily's father. Fran's . . . what? Impregnator. Why on earth had she kept the recording? Her portable accusing ghost? Suddenly, Dominic wanted to hear it again. He rewound the tape, started playing. After a few moments, he snapped it off. That voice! So helpless and dangerous!

He started to browse through Fran's papers. It was pointless, this search for clues, but he did not want to stop. He found a kind of journal written in several exercise books. It contained a recently written essay on words and what appeared to be her autobiography. Dominic lay down on the bed and read it with shock, over and over again. Can this be true? he wondered.

He understood her now. He knew what made her tick, what made her sick!

He knew why she could not remain in his well-lit well-off abode. It was too much a replica of her childhood home.

We should never have taken pity on her, he thought. Should have left her brooding in that slum. He knew what those tenements were like. He had lived once in a place like that until the atmosphere of slow decay drove him out. It was when he was a student in Glasgow. A house full of misfits living on their meagre incomes and wits. No scope, no hope. Yes, he knew the dank corridors, the smells of disinfectant and loneliness. The dowdy, genderless creatures who scurry past, head down, fearing your hello like an assault. And he could picture Fran living quite successfully in such a set-up. Perched five floors above the rest of humanity in a little fortress-attic. Throwing up her 'Nothing human can touch me' screen if she should bump into anyone. Zooming secretly in on other people with her merciless lens. Shielding herself with her writing. WORDS: an anagram of SWORD. 'You have a bent for writing,' he had told her one day. 'Bent?' she said, grinning, and he conceded: 'Oh, all right, talent.' But now he understood that she had liked the word with its suggestion of crookedness, deformity. She loved to discuss the turbid origins of art, the brilliance that can flower from psychic mutilation.

Oh, she was far too emotional, possessed of too strong a sense of doom, individual and global disaster.

'You love your doom!' he said aloud.

Yes, they should never have enticed her out of her dark corner. How wrong to think she would welcome an oasis. She could only take comfort when she thought she had no further to fall. Her allegiance was to the dark tenements, the dark places, the cold wilderness of Greenham Common, anywhere where there could be no forgetting of the real world and its countless trapdoors into madness and death.

Where are you, my doomed girl?

Why was it that just when you started to know someone, just when you were on the brink of . . . just when you might start to care, they went away?

'It must be getting late,' he realised, rising to light the lamp. There was a sound of voices and laughter outside on the street. Dominic went to look out of the window.

The darkening glass gave back his own face.

14

Fran's Story

My mother was in bed forever. She was into ailments in a big way. Mysterious afflictions, exhaustion, nervous prostration, aches and pains 'everywhere', pallor, hints of hellish thoughts. Sometimes her gentle enfeeblement escalated into frightening illnesses. An infection of the eyes which made her unable to bear light.

'I do not want to see.' And then years of self-starvation. 'I do not want to be.'

I could do lots of things from an early age. There was no point in cute-faced helplessness, so before I started school, I could dress myself, make tea, initiate and sustain conversations even in the face of her dogged silence. The only thing I couldn't cope with was my prized yard-long hair 'just like Mummy's'. The truth was that it resembled hers only in its superfluous length. Mine was wispy, fine and mousy. Hers was abundant, burnished brown, wavy, miraculous. She was Ophelia drowning in silk sheets and goose down. Like everything about me, my hair was meant to draw comparison with hers, and to suffer in comparison.

When I started school my life was full of chores; I had to get up earlier and earlier. My main morning ordeal was the daily comb out of the mass of knots and snarls my hair had accumulated during the night. My favourite story was the one about the princess imprisoned in the tower who escapes by plaiting her hair into a rope ladder!

'Can't I have it cut, please, please,' I used to plead on Mother's verbal occasions.

'Don't whine.'

'All the other girls have short hair.'

'You have to suffer to be beautiful.'

No one suffered more than my mother. No one was more beautiful.

I began to neglect the tortuous grooming of my hair, simply pulling it into a pony tail, brushing rigorously a couple of times a week. She told me a story, a 'true' story, about a factory girl who couldn't be bothered to release her hair from its elaborate chignon each night. She kept the pins and clips in and sprayed the hair every morning with hair lacquer. She began to have sensations and then agonizing pains in the head. Died screaming in madness and torment. After which it was discovered that earwigs had nested in her hair and had burrowed through her scalp to the brain.

'Can you imagine those nasty insects nibbling away at her? And all because she was too lazy to brush her hair!'

That put paid to my painsaving strategy and several nights' sleep.

My father had to give me a shampoo once a week. He would cradle my skull while he saturated the hair, then knead and massage my scalp so deliciously that tears burned my eyes and my breath rose from a far down part of my chest. I loved his hands, the tapering clever fingers, the hair covering the knuckles ('like a monkey' my mother said, sometimes laughing, sometimes not). But I worried about germs. My mother said he had made her ill. She was never ill before she met him.

After he rinsed away the soap, we went downstairs, no longer whispering, because now she wouldn't be able to hear. He could get the brush through the tangles in no time at all.

'There you are,' he would say. 'Will that be all, Madam?'

'No, I'd like a cut please. And a fringe.'

'Ah well, that requires the proper authorisation.'

He was a civil servant, working for the 'government' in Belfast Castle. I told him my problems about school. Mad teachers, mean 'friends', boring difficult lessons. In turn, he told me about his work, where the English lorded it over the Irish. The English were snobs, inept layabouts who overrated themselves and looked down their noses at everybody else. The only Englishman my father admired was Enoch Powell. 'A man of vision.'

'What's vision?' I asked.

'The ability to see clearly. And to imagine something better,' he said.

I had to go to my mother's room at least twice a day, before and after school. The curtains stayed drawn to banish sunlight and 'spies'. She lay there like an Egyptian queen in her burial chamber surrounded by her favourite possessions: a cringing chihuahua in the crook of her arm, a radio, books, women's magazines, sweets, medicines, cosmetics, scents, a mirror. Morning and afternoon I had to take her bug-eyed pet for a 'walk', so that he could 'fulfil his natural functions.' 'Don't tire him out!' she would say. He wasn't allowed to shit in the garden so I had to take him out in public. Her miniature ornamental excuse for a dog. Until he rolled his bulging eyes, squatted down and deposited his miniature ornamental faeces on the immaculate pavement. When I delivered him back after these brief excursions, his mistress greeted him as if he had been on some perilous odyssey.

On my way home from school each day, I rehearsed what I would say to her, trying to forge some amusing anecdotes out of the day's non-events, trying to remember or invent jokes. I knew she liked me to be merry, although she gazed at me like someone beyond all human emotion while I quipped and shook the bed with laughter and acted my age. 'My little clown,' she would say. 'I'm glad you're so happy. So full of life.' She seemed to need constant evidence of my joy. Proof that the stain of her sadness did not spread beyond the bed's edge. Providing it exercised my ingenuity to the hilt.

I preferred the times when she wanted me to massage her with oils and lotions. Embalming fluid. She loved to be caressed and touched but never to return the favour. It was on one of those days that I cracked, just that once. We had quarrelled when I asked her why we couldn't go on a holiday together, Daddy, Mummy, and me.

'I don't want to. You only think of yourself!'

'Maybe you would get on better with Daddy, if . . .'

'No, I wouldn't. Don't interfere. There are some things you won't understand until you get married.'

'I'll never get married. I'll stay and look after you!'

'Do you think I can afford to provide for you all your life?'

I offered to massage her then, trying to earn my keep. She lay with her eyes closed, lips gently apart, while I soothed sweet scented lotion into her legs and feet. I was working on her foot, the clean square nails, the tender skin between her toes, the tracery of veins, the polished instep, her poor beautiful foot that took her nowhere, when sobs broke from me and I pressed my lips to her ankle.

'What on earth . . .! Don't! You're tickling me!' I stopped, swallowed hard.

'Come here, if you want to kiss Mummy.' She puckered her lips, ready to plant a dry kiss on my brow, but I plunged my head into her chest. She held me for five minutes, while I stuck out my tongue at the displaced Bug Eyes.

Sometimes I would go into my father's room when he wasn't there. There was a Union Jack on the wall, books all over the floor. He left coins lying about carelessly. I took them. His wallet was there occasionally, full of cards and papers which meant he was important. He had a wardrobe with a sliding door and I liked to climb in there and sit in the enclosed darkness underneath the bitter tweed and sweat smell of his clothes. His parents were dead but my other grandparents lived near us. They had separate rooms as well. Later when I discovered that my friends' parents slept not only in the same room but in the same bed, I thought it must be some low class aberration enforced by lack of space or sense. I told myself stories inside the wardrobe. That's what led to my discovery. One day I screamed to the point of fainting when I heard Old Ma Cassidy outside hobbling along on her stick, muttering her curses to herself. It was my mother playing a trick, pretending to be one of the local tinkers.

'That'll teach you to hide,' she said.

It did.

My mother was convinced that I had inherited her frailty. There was a taboo on exercise and 'excitement'. Even so, I was ill all the time. Flu, colds, sinusitis, anaemia, perforated eardrums, allergies to dust, feathers, cats, pollen, and sunlight. Headaches mild and severe, sometimes both at the same time. Fainting spells, vomiting attacks, colitis. Nightmares and bed-wetting. Neuralgia every spring for four years running. Even on a good day, pins and needles at the very least.

With puberty, pain found another zone.

I was eleven when I started to bleed from that unnameable place. My mother told me it was something girls and women have to put up with. It meant you have to be 'careful'. And not let boys 'get personal' or do anything 'rude'. I thought it was an illness, arbitrary and painful as any other, but more alarming and humiliating.

There was a compensation that year, however. Amazingly, my parents bought me a horse. A tall beautiful brown horse, housed in stables near our home. Perhaps it was a signal to the neighbours: 'See how rich we are!' My mother chose the name Sultan for him. But I called him Rory. After I learned to ride, I was allowed to canter round the fields on my own. It was great. My sickening hair was all coiled and scraped inside a hat like a Sikh warrior's. My spine was perfectly straight. The moving muscular platform of Rory's back was beneath me. I was a horseman. I was like God. My version of God wasn't the usual fat old grandad dribbling his promises and threats down to earth. My God looked like a film star in a sultry rage. He had black furious eyes and red trousers. I imagined my own eyes like his as I sped along on Rory, shouting out all the proscribed words: 'spit, pee, bum, bosoms, cock . . .' And sometimes I would mock my own sycophantic lady's companion voice: 'How are you today, Mummy? I love you, Mummy . . . Shall I rub you anywhere? Shall I rub you out, out, out! Rub-a dub-dub!' One day I left Rory back in the stables and decided to go home by the fields instead of the road. I saw a man. He froze at the sight of me the way an animal does when you trespass on its lair. Then he approached slowly, baring his teeth in a sort of smile. He stood in front of me forcing me to stop.

'Been riding?' he said.

'Yes.'

'What does it feel like, eh, up there on the big gee-gee?'

'Have you never ridden a horse?'

He laughed nastily. 'Not a horse, no. Never a horse.' He kneeled down on the ground, alarming me. It was the way men knelt to propose in old films. He plucked a thick stalk of grass, bisected it with his thumbnail and started to chew the sappy edge. His face was ordinary, pale eyes, fat nose.

'I'm late for my lunch,' I said.

'Yes, works up the appetite, a nice ride.'

And suddenly his hands were rubbing my crotch and buttocks. He was panting like a bull.

'Any wee hairs there yet? Let's have a little looksee.'

I opened my mouth to scream and no sound came out. I wanted to see my father coming towards us. I couldn't believe that my father would not magically appear. I started to wave, pretending to see him and then I heard myself shouting: 'Dad! Dad!'

The man turned to look and I fled.

The mistake was to tell my parents. My mother hit me, then my father hit me because she cried. I was sent to bed, where I listened to them screaming at each other. He called her a 'professional cripple'. She said he was useless as a father as well as a husband. He wasn't a man. Finally they got around to complaining about me. I wandered about so fancy-free. I hadn't a thought in my head. I was always bringing attention to myself. My father came to see me later, bringing me some hot chocolate. He looked distraught. He warned me against men. Some men were animals, he said, lusting without limit. They wanted to 'break into' young girls. They wanted to hurt women. Even nice men could turn dangerous without warning. He made it sound as if molesters were hiding behind every tree. I had only a rudimentary understanding of sex. I had never seen a penis, although I knew it was some kind of connective tubing instrumental in the transfer of sperm to eggs. I had no idea that this process could be anything more than a tedious marital task. My father scared me. And I was puzzled. Surely my father was a good man, not crazed with urges to 'break into' girls and hurt women. Why didn't my mother love him, then? Why was she always moaning that he wasn't a 'man'? For a few weeks I was only allowed to go riding at weekends with my father watching over me. He became more and more impatient at the obligation. Finally they sold Rory without telling me.

'You'll miss him, I know. But it's for the best,' my mother told me calmly.

'No, no!' I don't believe her. It isn't possible. I want to grab her dog and squeeze it to death. I want to strike her. I turn and topple her bottles of perfume to the floor. 'No, no, no!' With one bound, she is out of bed and twisting my hair, she pushes me to the bathroom and shoves me under the cold shower until I am forced to swallow my rage.

'That wasn't to punish you. Hysterics are dangerous.' I am powerless in the face of her size, her strength, her stupidity.

She will make it up to me, she says. She will buy me a present. I wonder what she will find to replace Rory? A stupid doll? A puny goldfish? A docile hamster?

She made me sleep with her that night, so that she could 'keep an eye' on me. I lay beside her and pierced my hymen with her fat fountain pen.

My indoors life recommenced. My mother had sporadic bursts of energy during my adolescence. She would rise at noon and spend hours in protracted ceremonies of dressing and facepainting punctuated with teabreaks. People called round. Cronies from the Animal Rights Group, the Discover Yourself Through Writing group, clients for her *I Ching* readings. After a brief phase of unilateral homage, most of her friends were either in voluntary full flight or being energetically blacklisted by my mother, who enjoyed nothing better than the composition of a batch of denunciatory letters.

She paid me to polish her shoes and iron her clothes. I was her little maidservant, observing everything, saying nothing. I read everything I could get my hands on. The Bible, the wrong end, especially the *Song of Songs*, the lovers competing to praise every inch of each other's body. It was my first intimation that the body could be something

97

better than a locked china cabinet. I read Camus, Sartre, Lawrence, Kafka, Joyce, Dostoyevsky, Freud, the whole male voice choir, before I was sixteen. My adopted ghost fathers gave me a vocabulary of attack, a habit of suspicion. There was poison in the cup too. Lawrence preaching that woman's destiny is the 'ecstasy of subjection', Freud's 'penis envy', Sartre's hatred of the female body. I repeated poems to myself like mantras. 'I will arise and go now and go to Innisfree' made my muscles tingle with readiness to take me up hill and down dale, over the fields and far away.

A man called one day when my mother was at the library. He was one of her animal-protecting colleagues.

'You look miserable,' he said. A man of vision.

'Is there anything I can do for you?' he offered. Upstairs he removed his clothes and I took his penis in my hand. It was like a bone wrapped in silk.

'You have the air of a forensic scientist,' he said.

'You needn't worry about any blood,' I said. 'I'm not a virgin.'

'Neither am I.'

I knew what to do from films, all the kissing and exclamations. I had to say 'O God, O God,' of course, not knowing my lover's name. The entire operation was completed in seconds.

'You were lovely,' he said as if I were a meal.

'I didn't like that very much.'

'Neither did I. We'll try again later.'

'My mother will be back soon from the library.'

'Oh, I can't manage two of you!'

I liked him. He was what my father called an unserious person. Nick. Twenty-three. I decided to marry him when I left school.

Mother and I fell in love at the same time. She had acquired a psychiatrist and lived for her weekly visits. Love made her hopeful and lively. She replenished her wardrobe. Dr Arnold Flint was the perfect companion for her. Listening intently to her roll call of grievances, stifling no yawn, passing no judgement, possessing no self of his own. Easy to forgive him for being squat, ugly. She began to refer to her new clothes as 'my trousseau'. She kept promising me new brothers and sisters. She planned to elope with the doctor. No obstacle would deter them. Any reminder that the doctor's smiles and knowing looks were doled out to any one who could afford his fees, only enraged her. 'You think no one could possibly love me!'

Nick and I were practising sex in the great outdoors. We had reached the point where coitus lasted slightly longer than a carcrash and sometimes afforded an approximation of pleasure. I think I would have done it lying on a bed of nails. Anything not to be like my mother, a forty year-old Sleeping Beauty awakened by anticipation of a frog's kiss.

Suddenly the euphoria collapsed. Mother rang the police and the newspapers one day, accused the doctor of using her in harmful drug experiments. Her nightdress became her daydress again. My grandfather died that month, calling attention to himself for the first time in years. He had been a pensive old man, smoking and dwindling in a corner. The good thing about him in my eyes was his lack of fear and loathing for Catholicism.

Once I had bought a tiny doll dressed as a nun from a market stall. When my grandmother spotted it, she was alarmed and started scolding my parents. The doll was unmistakable evidence of my impending heresy. My soul was in danger. My parents were lax, incompetent guardians.

Stella's face became more taut and aquiline, a sure sign she was about to lash out. But at whom?

'She'll be carrying rosary beads before you know it!' Granny predicted.

Suddenly Stella grabbed my doll and smashed it against the fireplace.

'Shut up, shut up, *shut up!*' she shouted as the head toppled.

The grownups stared at the decapitated toy, looking mildly puzzled as if this act of destruction were not satisfying enough.

'What did you break the wee girl's dolly for?' My grandfather was suddenly giving a rare speech. 'You could have taken its clothes off it! Aye, you could have stripped it. Stripped a nun, heh-heh!'

Stella sniffed. 'Anyway, it was only cheap rubbish. Made in Hong Kong.'

'Oh, not the Vatican?' Grandad said wickedly.

Death shocked my mother out of bed and into perpetual motion. The days were full of the sound of the phone ringing, her brisk efficient voice, her car backing out of the driveway. She bought us all sober expensive clothes for the occasion.

*

THE EVENT
DRAMATIS PERSONAE

*The Widow:*Large unwieldy body racked by sobs. She holds a twisted sodden handkerchief. Sitting down as always. She never seems to go anywhere, even to the bathroom. An immobile but immensely strong woman, full of dangerous serenity, destitute of humour. Never calls anyone by name, preferring to say 'Son', 'Daughter', 'Child', so that her every utterance reminds us of our status and obligations. An expert on the mind of God and the customs of the aristocracy. Favourite expressions: 'It's God's Will' and 'No lady would ever . . .' In her caste system, God and Jesus are at the top, followed by the Queen, then closely by herself. Next comes the Unionist Party and all 'born again' Christians, then Protestants including the most lapsed and renegade but excluding Anglicans ('Catholics in disguise'). Then follow all other colours and creeds in a descending scale down to the unspeakable bottom of the heap with its vast congregation of Catholics, Sinn Feiners, blacks, Jews, criminals, madmen, spermatozoa, germs, genitalia. Eyes pale blue like a sea captain's. Tears washing the disapproval out of them. Is it guilt that she feels?

Mother: No one could guess today her awful debility.
(Stella) She is the semi-orphan, dutiful daughter, her mother's consolation prize. See her dark stylish suit, her good taste shoes, her silver earrings flashing little beckoning spangles of light. In the crowded room, she is solitary, moving inside her clear intangible globe, filled with warm scent. See the inestimable grace of her body, the elsewhereness of her face. She is listening to distant melodies.

Father: Tall, gangling, handsome in a helpless assertive way. He is calm and courteous. An unknowing philistine. He thinks nothing is happening in this room. He thinks friendliness and laughter are nothing to be suspicious about. He thinks ideas are not real, words are of no consequence.

For the time being, my mother and father co-exist peacefully. They have hung up their rusty swords. But he stays away from her. They are always, in any room, a hundred and eighty degrees apart.

*

Myself: I am a Young Girl, starched collar, knees together, startled foal looks when someone speaks to me. I pass round tea and Kleenex with timid kindness. My body, which has no respect and no sense of occasion, is menstruating alarmingly. My pale ravaged face is much appreciated.

The Corpse: He is tastefully arranged for viewing in the front parlour, a room out of bounds when he was alive because of his habits of spilling food, burning holes in cushions and carpets with his careless ciggies, spitting in the fire and missing the target.

His wife refuses to allow the coffin lid to be closed. She is in love.

Uncle Frank: A member of that section of the family which my mother calls the Bucolics or the Crassettes. He is a bloated gnome got up in a rumpled suit. Loud nostalgic voice: 'What a shame, eh? One minute here, next minute, your number's up! What good does it do to worry, eh? Makes you think, eh? He wouldn't have wanted us to be miserable, I'm sure of that, God bless him!'

His wife, Florrie: A good name. Apt. Florid complexion. Floral dress. Flowery sentiments. She hands out sherry and tranquillisers to everyone.

'I knew something had happened, so I did, didn't I, Frankie? Because I was standing in the kitchen, and I felt somebody stroking my hair. I turned round and there was no one there! Half an hour later I got the news, so I did.'

Greedy as we are for evidence of ghosts, especially demonstrative ghosts, no one is impressed. If Grandfather felt like some belated tactile indulgence, would he choose her?

More aunts, uncles, distant cousins. Married or unmarried, how chaste they look. They believe in God and the Devil, Heaven and Hell, toil and frugality, thick savings accounts, curtains made to match. Burning only with Pentecostal fires, they sniff the air for the fumes of vice and moral blight. They police the room with their scolding stares, alert for nascent infidelities, stirring loins, salivating mouths, irreligious thoughts. They agree that my grandfather has gone to a Better Place; they are absolved from weeping.

They look severely at my grandmother. There is something

immoderate and blasphemous in her loud untidy grief. But they forgive her because they are Christians and she is only a woman.

I am ashamed in their presence. Of my blood-soaked tampon, the dirt I suddenly spy under my fingernails. Because I am an unrepentant whore.

We are going to have a party! The table is laden. A hock of ham, smoked salmon, salads, bread and butter, iced cakes. My father whispers that it is obligatory to provide a 'bit of a do' for the mourners, who need 'fortifying' after their walk to the cemetery.

'Do ye want to see the body?' says Cousin Rex, leering like a tout outside a Soho peepshow.

'No, thanks.'

'Aren't you going to pay your respects?' Disbelieving rebuke from Grandmother.

'I want to remember him as he was.'

'Go on, love,' says Florrie. 'It'll help you to realise that he's gone from us.'

Rex leads me into the shaded room. Bending over the coffin. It is Grandfather all right. It is his dappled bald head. The skin around his eyes has turned bluish. His nails look obscenely long. In death he is magisterial.

'There was a cockroach in here this morning,' Rex informed me.

'There are no cockroaches in this house.'

He gave a superior laugh. 'Oh no? Can't you guess why one might just poke its head out now?'

'Perhaps you brought it with you. Perhaps it's your pet.'

'Aren't you going to give Grandaddy a kiss byebye?'

'No.'

'Go on, he won't bite.'

'You're sick!'

'Kiss me better, then,'

'Fuck off.'

His hand clamps the back of my neck, he pushes me forward, pressing my face close to Grandad's. The smell! Wet rotten fruit. A sweet swamp. O God! I stop breathing.

'Give in?'

I nod desperately, Rex releases me and I fling myself at him, kissing his mouth, sinking my teeth into his lower lip. He yelps. I run.

Weeping in the living room. 'I will never be bad again, never . . .' Convulsed in my mother's arms, gulping down her heartbreaking clean smell. 'Who let this child go in there?' she demands, eyes blazing. I do not tell her that my grandfather is reeking.

The interment. Heavy brutal thud of soil on the coffin. Back to the house. Hankies out of sight now, laughter unrestrained. Amazing anecdotes about my grandfather. He is transformed from a nuisance with no personality into a hero, generous to a fault, his life crammed with exciting escapades, his little failings all witty and endearing. I have never known him, never suspected there was anybody knowable dwelling inside him. The guests seat themselves at the banquet, ready to do justice to the gutbusting repast. They are happy, they are alive, alive, o!

They chomp and chop their way through cold meats and sweet pickles. They lick their lips, they pick their teeth, every now and then a belch breaches the peace. He is dead. He has entered mythology.

Grandmother dabs at her sore eyes. 'Do you think the rain will penetrate the soil? Do you think the coffin was thick enough?' She imagines him slumbering in damp hibernation on the hillside.

'What does it matter, Granny?'

'At the Second Coming, the dead will rise again. The Resurrection of the Body, it's been promised. That's why you mustn't be cremated.'

How could I control what would be done to my dead body? To my living body? I ran to the bathroom, everything in my stomach rising at the thought of the Last Day, rotting corpses flinging soil aside like blankets, standing up and stretching their white bones, the flesh hanging from them like defiled rags.

After the funeral, Stella and I were both sleepy, as if drugged. I lay on her bed looking at a framed photograph of her parents' wedding. My grandmother, eyes wide, mouth a stern line. She holds a snowy Bible and a huge bunch of lilacs. Looks as if she's saying: 'I'm twenty. It's time. I'm here.' Grandfather, a sweet perplexed youth, without bearings, without answers.

'If it hadn't been for you . . .' I told him silently.

'What was he like when you were a little girl?'

'What? Oh, he was so-so. A good provider.' She was staring at herself in the mirror, training a spotlight on her features, a violent illumination.

'My looks will last five more years,' she announced. 'Ten if I'm careful.'

'Then what? I suppose you'll wear a paper bag over your head!'

'I'm thinking of going back to my doctor,' she said pretend-casually.

'Oh Mummy, no!'

'It's quite a trauma, after all, losing one's father.'

'You can't tell him about Grandad.'

'Why ever not?'

'Because you already told him your parents were dead, remember! You made up yarns about everything! You didn't want him to think you came from a poor family.'

'Through no fault of my own!'

'Why be ashamed of your background? Jesus was born in a stable!'

'He had other advantages.'

'I suppose you're going to be "in love" again, mooning around, staring through everybody?'

'It's not "in love", don't be childish! It's called "positive transference" and I should have stayed with the doctor to work through it. He'll let me come back. And he'll understand my little prevarications. He knows the human heart. Nothing can shock him. After all, I wouldn't need him if I weren't so highly strung.'

'I need *you*.'

'You're sixteen.'

She creamed her face and wiped it with powder blue tissues. I watched her through my half-shut eyes, trying to imagine her in the doctor's office, inventing herself from scratch, eradicating all vulgarities, all failures. I wondered if I figured in her epic? As Fran? As Frances? Or even Francesca? 'My darling child. The solace of my bitter life. My millstone. I would have left him years ago if only . . . I could have been a painter/explorer/tap-dancer. I would have found my true love, my twin soul, someone worthy, equal. My daughter is so like me, Doctor, you've no idea, so sensitive and gifted. She's so like him, Doctor, boorish and phlegmatic. Naturally, they conspire against me . . .'

'. . . and so I have no choice,' she was saying. I hadn't heard her start to speak.

'If you had to choose between kissing a dead man or a dirty horrible boy, what would you do?' I asked her.

'What an unhealthy imagination!'

I jumped up and took her cloak from the wardrobe, wrapped it round myself, then hauled her suitcase from under the bed.

'Where are you going?' she sounded alarmed.

'Impersonations,' I explained. It was one of our ritual games, but I had never played her before. It was understood between us that she was not imitable, not ridiculous. 'Doctor, dear, I've brought the money.' I dragged the suitcase over to the bed as if it weighed a ton. 'Will that suffice? I think you ought to know that I'm in love with you, Doctor. I have conceived this terrible lust. It rules my life. Despite the fact, the lamentable fact, of your runtish appearance. You mean, this is progress? This is . . . normal! I cry all day. My life is empty, Doctor . . . You're sure? A good sign. And I can keep paying, I mean, coming . . .?'

I thought she would rush at me, fists flying. But she sat there like a kicked spaniel. 'Don't use that word "lust" ', she said finally. 'It makes you sound common.'

'Would you look at the legs on her!' Stella whispered.

'Why can't we go home, Mum? I've got work to do, for school.'

She went on peering through the rain-stippled windscreen at a woman emerging from a car parked on the opposite side of the road. There was nothing remarkable about her. Just the usual suburban woman laden with bags of shopping.

'What a rear end! I'd never let myself get like that. Those poor things!'

'What? What poor things?'

'Those children of hers. They look so pale.'

I examined the profiles of the two snobby-faced girls who had climbed out of the back seats.

'They look stuck-up to me.'

The flawed trio disappeared into their house, while Stella continued to watch avidly as if the curtains and trailing plants in the window might yield up some vital secret.

'Why are you being so nosey?' I asked. Usually my mother treated other people as tedious ancillaries, insubstantial to the point of transparency. Why this alarming interest in the circumference of a stranger's bum?

'Are we going to sit here all day?'

She drove away in silence, abruptly broken by her comment: 'Their house was surprisingly ordinary, wasn't it?'

'Looked all right. Same as any other house.'

'My point exactly,' she spoke with satisfaction, then with doubt: 'I suppose she does look more like a wife than I do?'

'Who is she? What does a wife look like?'

'Oh, you know, a *wife*.'

'I don't know.'

'Sort of cosy and worried at the same time.'

'That's a mum, isn't it?'

'Oh yes, you're right.'

'Whose wifely wife is she?'

Stella flashed me a glorious raffish smile.

'Oh Mummy, no! Not the bloody shrink's wife! You trailed her home!'

'No, of course not! I just happened to see her car, *his* car in front of me. Anyway, why shouldn't I know more about him? He knows everything about me! Tit for tat.'

'God, I hope you don't use that expression in front of him!'

'Why?'

'He's a follower of Fraud, isn't he? I'm a Reichian myself.'

No response.

'Mum.'

'What?'

'What do you think of Wilhelm Reich?'

'Never heard of him.'

'He said that ecstasy . . . *physical* ecstasy is the cure for all personal and social ills.'

'Physical ecstasy?'

'Orgasm.'

She frowned.

'An orgasm a day keeps the doctor at bay,' I chirped.

Tears pelted out of her eyes. 'O Arnold,' she wept.

'He's not worth it, Mum! . . . Oh, stop the car! We'll crash!'

'So what?'

'I am your daughter, you know! Flesh of your flesh. Don't I count?' But I knew the answer. Dr Fraud was the only person who could penetrate her magnificent indifference. Only a diamond can cut a diamond. My father no longer seemed to care about Stella, no longer gave her timid lovesick looks. She had almost stopped eating. I began to worry when I saw her bones gleaming behind her skin. I tried to talk to him about it. 'Can't you do something? Don't you think she's making herself ill?'

He inspected his nails.

'Dad?'

He was staring into the distance. His voice when he spoke was full of a kind of voluptuous regret. 'Mad bitch,' was all he said.

Stella's inarticulate rage and the troubles in the country both aroused my father's bewildered resentment. He kept himself always within earshot of radio or television news: they punctuated his days. We had fought bitterly since the beginning of the Civil Rights struggle in 1968. When Protestants burned out Bombay Street on the Falls Road, destroying Catholic homes, he had denied their involvement. Protestants would never do anything so lawless and vicious. The Catholics had burned their own homes; they would do anything to incriminate Loyalists. In the next breath, he said: 'Anyway, those Fenians got off lightly. Nobody touched a hair of their heads. If it had been the IRA attacking us . . .' His selective grief and moral confusions made me despise him.

I remember one beautiful evening watching dusk fall on our garden. The highest branches of the trees silhouetted against the pale gold sky. Smoky wings of moths fluttered in the hedges. The deadly bulletin blaring from the television seemed incredible. How could a gun battle take place a mile from where we sat? It was like news from Mars. My father must have sensed or shared my mood. He came and placed his hand on my shoulder and said: 'It used to be the loveliest wee country in the world.' He mourned it like the dissolution of a private kingdom.

On Bloody Sunday he cheered at the news of British troops killing thirteen demonstrators in Derry. 'Slap it into them.'

'They're just marchers, Dad! Some of them are only my age!'

'They're enemies of the state.'

'Then so am I. I agree with them.'

'That's right. Bite the hand that feeds you.'

'Feeds me because of my chance denomination! Shoots other people's children dead! Just for demanding equality!'

'That's a ploy. They want to get their hands on this country.'

'They want it *back*.'

Nick was my relief, my occasion for laughter. I was seventeen and he was twenty-four but looked younger. He was small and spritely, full of warmth that never boiled over into fury. His face was the sort that only a sane and balanced person would fall in love with.

He let me regale him with the follies of my parents and squawked with delight at my father's barbarity and my mother's implacable joylessness.

'What's *wrong* with them?' he would say.

He was the only Irish person I knew who possessed no rhetoric, no guilt, no hatred. The nearest thing to a nurturing elder brother, albeit incestuous, that I could have had. He talked about everything, making room for my doubts, which were unwelcome in my school, the sort of institution where an exploring intelligence or even talkativeness were considered subversive.

Religion made Nick laugh. The idea that we would spend eternity in perpetual roasting or floating in a vast blue boredom, the singing of hymns our sole recreation. Disbelief in the next world attached him firmly to this one and he wanted to see as much of it as possible. India, Mexico, Africa . . . dreams sewn together out of travelogues, novels, geography lessons and longings for *somewhere else*. The natural world filled him with curiosity and reverence. He could name the stars and the birds from their cries, even rare ones like the corncrake. He was the patron and defender of vermin and creepy-crawlies. Once when I was sitting on a fallen tree, I flinched as something moved under my hand and looked down to find insects pouring out of the crumbling bark. Blobs of grey jelly on blind rushing feet.

'Kill them! Kill them!' I screamed, but Nick only laughed and gently led me away.

'We were trespassing in *their* world. It would be different if they were chewing up your house.'

I was ashamed of my horror of certain creatures, considering it a 'womanly' enfeeblement, but everything that crawled or slithered or exuded slime was the stuff of my nightmares.

I was becoming ashamed of a lot of things. My cashmere sweaters, my leather gloves, my supreme good fortune. Journalists and research-ers were flocking to Belfast at that time, dissecting the violence, highlighting the poverty in rundown areas. Television images would stay with me all day. Faces full of strain, anger, weariness. Stories I could not forget. A nine year-old girl in Divis Flats prescribed Valium after waking one morning to find two rats gnawing her finger. At the same time as this guilt and need to understand were growing in me, another voice ran its commentary in my head: 'It's their own fault. They breed like rabbits. You couldn't give them decent housing, they'd wreck it in a day. It's all propaganda . . . It's really the Church of Rome that keeps them back . . .' And sometimes I uttered these shibboleths like a ventriloquist's dummy. Or did I really believe them? Sometimes hate gave me a good feeling, like sucking sweets under the covers in bed. I already knew that a penitent rich girl, a tormented liberal is something clownish and lonely.

Nick would rarely discuss the political strife. He was not plugged in to it. There were no soldiers on our streets, no hooded bodies to be discovered at dawn. His neutrality angered me.

'But you must have some opinion! You must want somebody to win? What kind of future do you want to see?'

'Win?' he smiled. 'As far as I can see, we have no future. Only a past, constantly re-enacted. Correction. This country has no future. But we're another matter.' And he started to sing: 'Come live with me and be my love . . .'

He told me a story once about a Russian called Peter Ouspensky. One day in the middle of the First World War this man saw two huge lorries loaded high as houses with new wooden crutches. There was something chillingly evil about such methodical provision of mountains of crutches for legs not yet severed. And yet they were made and despatched by nice, normal men and women, not lunatic robots.

'Can you imagine,' Nick said, 'all the planning and industry that went into producing those crutches and getting them from A to B? Once something evil starts, it's easy to channel effort into serving it, but not into stopping it! It's going to be like that here. Violence, retaliation, funerals. People will be swept along. The gunmen think they're in control. But _it_ is.'

'It?'

'Evil.'

'You talk about it as if it's . . . you know, a thing on its own. An entity. Like the Devil.'

He laughed. 'I believe in human unreason.'

'Original Sin?'

'Use your own labels, if you like. If they are your own?'

The places we went — the seaside, the Mourne Mountains, the pubs. Not in Belfast where the doors were guarded and strangers suspect and the atmosphere a mixture of determined merriment and tight wrath, but out in the countryside where the bombers didn't go, not yet, and no one eyed us with distrust. Those were the nights I loved, roasting my knees near the coal fire, nursing a glass of something unfamiliar and sophisticated: brandy or Black Bush whisky. All around us in the early evening there would be raucous laughter, shouted conversations. Sometimes I overheard men bragging about their or someone's exploits against . . . who?

'He was about to plug the wee bastard, so he was. But he shot himself in the friggin' foot!'

They were full of conspiratorial grins, impenetrable jargon, hee-hawing.

Could they be . . .? No, they were just ordinary men, of course, recycling and embellishing tales they had heard. Surely no one really involved could talk about those deadly acts as if they were high jinks?

'Is this a Protestant pub or a Catholic pub?' I sometimes asked.

'This is a drinking pub,' Nick would always insist. Sometimes strangers let their eyes linger on me. A gleam of truculent desire. A look of sweet wistfulness. I loved it.

Usually there would be a group of musicians playing and sooner or later people would join in the singing. They would start off with rollicking foot-stomping numbers but the end of the evening always heralded tearful melodies that tightened my throat. There was something forlorn and irremediable and exquisite about those sounds that connected with the landscape outside, with the low hills, the mist, the thwarted but undying hopes. I thought I was close to 'Irishness' and I longed to be 'proper' Irish.

My secret meetings with Nick were making me anxious. I lied about where I was going. Not so much from fear of being forbidden to see him as out of habit and to preserve my privacy. But we were bound to be discovered. Nick decided he should become my Official Boyfriend.

'There's no reason to sneak about. You're seventeen.' So I plucked up courage and asked permission to 'date' him. Nick and his family were slight acquaintances of my parents, so at least they had no qualms about his pedigree.

'Oh him!' Stella said. 'He has no personality.'

'Hmmm, still waters,' Dad said. 'I want to see this fella.'

Nick called at the house a few days later. I was proud of him. He did not call my father 'Sir'. He did not give Stella a shit-eating grin. He was unquelled by her languid self-possessed beauty. He was there for *me*. The failure of her power surprised her, I could tell by her downturned mouth. My father's glasses slipped down his nose and he peered over them like an elderly judge.

'And where do you propose to spend your time? The cinemas are deserted.'

'I thought we might go to things in the Students' Union,' Nick said. 'Debates and films.'

'No bars,' my father stipulated. 'Remember, lad, I know your people! Your father's a Masonic colleague of mine. You make sure you take good care of my girl!'

Nick's idea of looking after me was to keep a stock of rubbers in his glove compartment. My parents never suspected my advanced sexual life. Although Nick was a postgraduate student with a driver's licence and an electric razor, they referred to him always as 'that boy of yours'. Asexual. Harmless.

My parents' easy trust gave Nick misgivings.

'Your father would lynch me if he knew!'

'I know. But it's like burgling his house or trespassing in his garden. I'm just another piece of his property. Anyway, they have no idea. They think it's only my mind that you're corrupting!'

'What do you mean?'

'Oh, every time I say something they don't like, they accuse me of quoting you. They imagine I'm too dumb to have my own opinions.'

'No. Your father told me you have a first-rate mind.'

'Chip off the old block! He thinks of it as a sort of tape-recording of mathematical formulae and Latin verbs.'

I had no guilt about sex then. Because of my mother and Wilhelm Reich, I associated rectitude with insanity. That winter of 1973 Nick and I made love in the car. The silence and the steamed windows turned it into a cocoon, cut off from the world's judgement. What comes back to me now are the smells. The fragrant leather of the seats, Nick's breath like apples after drinking cider, the brackish odour of sex. He loved my body; he made me feel all right about it, especially *down there*, that nameless place that bled and peed and juiced up with desire. The inner lips still looked to me like the red raggedy combs on roosters' heads but Nick said that inside was like wet immaculate silk lapping against him. In the cramped conditions that gave us pins and needles, we were as leisurely as married lovers in a deep bed, arousing each other and waiting until the point of excruciation. Sometimes it was love that I felt, other times an unpredictable dark terror that wanted only to press itself flat against a man. Any man.

Afterwards we sat and talked, watching the moon slip in and out of focus through the streaming windows. I hated the journey home. Vigilantes were out in force on Newtownards Road which we had to pass through. Men in parkas, hoods with cut-out eyes over their faces, standing behind their makeshift roadblocks.

'There's nothing to worry about with our Prod names and our Prod destination,' Nick said.

'They're scary all the same.'

I survived each school day only by wondering how I was going to manage to sit through it. Row after row of girls in white socks and white collars. Most of the teachers were well practised in perpetual monologue. Question and answer periods were the briefest exchanges. Sometimes the young teachers seemed more girlish and animated than us. They were the ones who would get suddenly vexed with our nullity, slam their books shut and plead: 'What do you have to say? What do you really think? Do you think?'

I didn't mind being bullied by teachers. They were maternal; there was a kind of love in their desire for excellence, and anyway, they could not keep it up relentlessly. Unlike some of their students.

I had escaped the attentions of the bullies in the early years. My asthma attacks warded off all others. Good marks often earned unpopularity, but mine were more of a stigma because I was an unconcealed Swot, one of the lower and highly ignorable forms of life.

Everything changed after Jilly Martin saw me out with Nick. *Sotto voce* conversations started to take place behind my back.

'It's got a mannikin!'

'Ooh, wonders will never cease!'

'Who is it? Anyone we *know*?'

'Nickie . . .'

'Yes? Come on, we can't guess who would fancy It!'

'Nickie Fitzpatrick.'

'Oh, I know him! He's had everybody, even married women . . .'

'That's why he's scraping the bottom of the barrel now.'

'Scraping the bottom of something!'

They pretended to fall about with laughter.

'Ask It! Ask It!'

'What's it like, It? Do you play with him?'

'I know, they play battleships!'

'Leave me alone!'

'Ooh, that's not very nice!'

'It looks different, doesn't It? They say that happens when you surrender.' She made a great mouthful out of the word.

'Yes, It looks mucky.'

112

'Mucky, mucky, mucky,' they chanted.

'Did it hurt?' It was the first time Monica had opened her mouth.

'Did it hu-rt?' Jilly squeaked in four ascending semitones.

'He won't respect you any more,' Monica assured me. Why not, I thought. I still respect him.

One day I opened my desk to find 'HOOR' scratched on the inside lid and a well-thumbed magazine placed on top of my papers. A pornographic magazine. I hid it in my bag. At home I made tea and cheese sandwiches. Stella was downstairs, chatting happily on the phone. There was something about her today that made me scrutinise her. Something feathery and radiant despite the blatant too-red mouth, the weighty gold bracelets.

'Mum,' I called out as she replaced the receiver.

'Hello, my Darling.'

'You look cheerful all of a sudden.'

'Yes, yes, yes!'

'Mum, you're not going anywhere, are you? You wouldn't go away?'

'You know I've been an idiot! I didn't see . . . worrying all the time about failure . . . a failed marriage. I mean, why should it be *my* failure? Most men, you know, they have no feelings, no imagination. They're barely human. And they blame their impotence on us, on *us*!' She laughed with delight, then turned very grave:

'I tell you this, Darling, so that you don't waste your life. The way I have. But not any more.'

'What are you up to now?'

'Don't frown. You look like a traffic warden. Yes, I am going to University! I'm not going to mope and stagnate any more. It was Arnold's brainwave. He says I need an outlet for my creativity, my self-expression.'

'But I'm going to University next year!'

'Won't it be super? We'll be like sisters. Everyone says we look like sisters, anyway! It'll be our private joke!'

I noticed that the cheese I was eating was discoloured in places, hard as soap. I threw it back on to the plate.

'I've got work to do upstairs,' I said.

'Yes, work. Work's the thing,' she said absent-mindedly.

In my room I began to study the magazine. The readers' letters. A man who could not get an erection unless his wife wore a binliner. One who said he had trained his spaniel to lick his wife into a frenzy and 'prepare' her. Another who liked nothing better than to eat chocolate mousse out of his girlfriend's vagina.

'I'll go away,' I decided. 'Study in England. Or abroad.'

A broad. A word for a bad woman. Hoor. Tart. Slag. *He's had everybody, even married women . . .*'

The centre section of the magazine consisted of pictures. Men and women, their limbs enmeshed like professional wrestlers. So many undreamed of positions. Women straddling men, lying aslant men. Kneeling like dogs. A woman's mouth straining, yearning towards a dewy penis. The man standing, the woman crouching at his feet. Anonymous legs spread to show a purple gash and a gaping anus.

The most horrible part of these women was their faces. Or their face. It was a shared face. A near-moronic expression. Docile, yet cunning, knowing. I went and washed my hands as if a smell of taint had seeped from the pages. But then I returned to look at the pictures again.

Wanton. Wanting.

I kept thinking about my parents, sure that this sensual alphabet contained clues to their battle with each other. I regretted my sudden access to this knowledge. It aroused in me a belated modesty. Love and sex, sex and freedom, separated in my mind. What had those calculated techniques to do with love? What was free about those grovelling, glaze-eyed women?

Did I really look different the way Jilly said? Did I, would I, look like them?

After that I shoved Nick away from me or made love viciously, marking him with my nails. I questioned him till we were both tired and bored, but I couldn't stop. He disrespected me, he took me for granted, he thought I was a slut: I presented him with collected proofs. How many girls had he fucked? How many was he still fucking?

'I've never "fucked" anyone! Don't talk to me like that!'

'Why not? That's the word for it, isn't it? That's the name of what we do!'

'Less and less.'

'Find someone else, then.'

'I don't want to, for God's sake! Get it through your head, I don't want to!'

I wanted him to: I would be unable to bear it if he did. He started to talk about spending the approaching summer in New York on a working holiday. I didn't believe it. New York was high temperatures, cockroaches, crimewaves, and severance from me. But he kept up the idea, and I thought he was trying to make me worry about losing him. After all, what could be more aphrodisiac than a departing back? Then I really did get worried. I decided that his travel plans were his way of signalling the end of our relationship, of easing himself out of it. We would be apart for four months. Separation would become natural, a fact.

But Nick was defeated by all the practicalities of such a venture. He simply could not go about the business of obtaining a passport and a visa, of finding out about flights, accommodation, possible jobs. I don't know why. Maybe it was the incapacity of a bar-room dreamer. Maybe it was the violence all around us that made so many people live strictly a day at a time, that induced such a numbness of spirit.

I was glad that he stayed. And then I was sorry.

The bomb would have missed him by a continent if . . . If if if. If he had gone to New York, if he had stayed home that day, if he had taken a different turning, if he had bumped into a friend and gone for a drink . . . 1974. Nick's last year. The one with only six months in it.

One minute he is walking past a pub, next minute he is dying in the explosion. My mother told me. A June evening. A shaft of amber sunlight across my bed. Me sitting by the window, thinking idly. She entered and paused in the doorway, looking so stricken, even her hair seemed paralysed with thought.

'What? Is something wrong?'

'My poor, poor child.'

'Daddy!'

She shook her head slowly. 'Your friend Nick. He's been . . . There was a bomb blast.'

'No!'

'Ardagh Street. A pub. He was outside, but still . . .'

'Where is hc? I've got to go!'

'No, love. Please. He's dead.'

I remembered it then, the dull crump I had heard in the afternoon. I remembered thinking: 'That's only a two or three pounder.'

She stayed with me all night, holding my hand, rocking me, telling me my future. She said that the young heal fast, that I would fall in love with many others, that Nick would become a sweet fading memory. She said that he had died instantly with no pain, no horror. I couldn't cry or speak. I wanted out of that room as if his death were true only in that place where it had been spoken.

By dawn we were both headachy with strain and sleeplessness.

'Will it be on the news?' I whispered. I wanted to hear a refutation. It was a case of mistaken identity. She nodded and we went downstairs to listen to the radio. The tally was announced: three dead, eight injured, two seriously. One of the dead was Nicholas Fitzpatrick, a twenty-four year-old research student. Loud, clear, and implacable. A fact.

No one claimed responsibility. Later there were rumours and counter-rumours: it was a sectarian attack by Protestants, a revenge bombing. It was an IRA 'own goal'. Some suspected the SAS and spoke of all kinds of murky gains they could make from such an action. The next few days passed somehow. No tears would come. No sleep.

I went for long walks all over the city, no longer afraid of the 'troubled' areas, no longer bothering to look to the left and to the right.

There was no such thing as a safe area, I knew that now. No place of safety. All the futile little rules of self-protection ticker taped through my head: Do not sit on the seat of a public lavatory. Do not stand under a tree in a thunderstorm. Breathe through your nose in crowded places. Beware of strangers. I tried over and over again to imagine Nick on that final day. What time did he rise? Did he feel cheerful or sad? What did he eat, read, think, say? Where was he going? Did he have a premonition? Did he die unknowingly? Did his whole life flash before his eyes? What was his 'whole life'?

I recomposed those hours with a desperate ingenuity as if by rewriting the start and middle of the story I could also transform its conclusion. He didn't die. Could not die. I went to the site of the bomb. Rubble everywhere. The pub door still absurdly intact and upright, standing somehow without support. There was no weight, no smell of death. The rain had rinsed away the blood.

I went to the cemetery and sat among the chrysanthemums in their slimy urns. I remembered the lorryloads of crutches for the not yet severed limbs. Was it preordained which limbs were lost? I imagined soldiers' bodies with perforations along the joins visible only to God's eyes.

There were people in Belfast who reacted with robust resignation to the hazards of bombs and bullets. 'If your name's on it . . .' they would say.

Was it Fate? God's Will? Some kind of celestial comment on Nick's political impartiality? Or on our illicit sex? I recalled my grand-mother's warning: 'God will take away what is most precious to you to bring you back to righteousness.'

My fault. Was it?

The funeral clothes came out again.

'You don't have to go, you know,' Mum said.

'I do. I'll never believe it otherwise.'

'Well, control yourself. You weren't his fiancée, remember.'

The coffin was closed. The 'body' was too destroyed to be exhibited. I imagined Nick charred, his flesh hanging in ribbons. My throat was so constricted I thought I would suffocate. Everyone looked stunned with sorrow. They reminded me of dull bewildered cattle. Except Nick's father. He was rage incarnate. Anger seemed to flow from his pores, hair, fingers.

'God bless you, Mr Fitzpatrick. Keep your heart up,' a young clergyman muttered.

'Aye!' The word was like a sharp sword. He sat chain-smoking, careless of the ash spilling down his jacket.

'What are you looking at, Miss?' he challenged me. 'Like what you see, do you? Fancy the older version?'

'Hush, Davey darling, you can't take it out on the young woman.' It was his sister. Mr Fitzpatrick stood up, making her spill the scalding tea she was proffering.

'Why couldn't it have been me?' he seemed to be addressing the window. 'Why?'

The rest of the day is a blurred nightmare, in which the headstone glares out.

In Memory
of
Our Beloved Son
JAMES NICHOLAS FITZPATRICK
1950–1974
Murdered by Terrorists
on the sixteenth day of June

The sun beat down throughout the ceremony, turning our black clothes limp. Through the haze of heat I thought I saw my parents embrace but I couldn't be certain. Back at Nick's house, Mrs Fitzpatrick spoke. Her whole face was chapped and haggard.

'So that's over and done with,' she said. 'Now there's only the rest of my life to get through! Why did you never come here before? He talked about you a lot.'

'Oh! Don't . . .'

'I'd like to give you something. A keepsake. Did you love my son?

117

Well, never mind that. I want to give you something whether you did or not.'

She handed me a watch, Nick's gold watch. 'Here, take it!'

'No.'

'Of course, my dear.'

I knew I would scream if I had to touch that watch. The woman looked dismayed.

'No! Please! I can't . . .'

Images flashed before me: Nick and I huddled in the back of the car, me lifting his wrist to check the time from the glowing numerals. The sound of ticking in my ear when he held me a certain way. My hands flew to cover my face. Suddenly my mother's light cool touch.

'I've just been waiting for her to crack all day!' she apologized. 'I really must get her home.'

It wasn't until months afterwards that I understood my instinctive hatred for that watch. It had more time than Nick. I did not want it sitting on my wrist murdering the minutes of my life also.

I discovered the grain of luxury at the heart of grief, the indifference to cleanliness, food, the future. I didn't turn up for my final 'A' level examinations. I wasn't going to University. I wasn't going to do anything. For a time my mother was sweetness itself, bringing me tea and snacks, but not nagging me to get up or eat or even talk. But after a few months she grew impatient.

'What do you do up there all day? Surely you *do* something! For crying out loud, are you trying to turn yourself into a memorial?' She tried to bribe me with presents.

'Wouldn't you like some driving lessons? Do you hear me?'

'No thanks.'

'Would you like your own television? Seeing as how you spend your entire life sequestered in your room!'

'I don't see the point of having two sets in the house.'

'Oh, you don't see the point of anything!'

Finally, my father was sent to 'deal' with me. I could hear him being primed for the interview. He knocked on my door and came cautiously into the room. His hair was falling over his eyes. It made him look young. He held a newspaper dangling behind his back.

'Fran?'

'Daddy?'

'That was only a taster, you know.'

'What?'

He lowered himself into the chair with a sigh.

'The boy. Nick. A taster. Of what life is like. Reality. It's hard, bloody hard. And you must be hard, too. Do you know what I'm saying?'

'Yes. Hard,' I whispered.

'You see, you can't fall at the first hurdle, can you? . . . Look at your mother! She can't stand . . . withstand anything, even a cold in the head! It's a miracle she ever gave birth to you, believe you me! Such a song and dance when she found out she was carrying you . . . She nearly . . .'

'Nearly what?'

'I thought you were different.'

'What did she nearly do? When she knew . . .'

'Oh, you know her. Antics. I thought you were different. Remember what a tough wee article you were?'

'Was I?'

'Not half! Do you mind the time you wrestled with that lad who uprooted the flowers out of our front garden? And twice the size of you!'

'I floored him!'

'You see, that's the spirit!'

'Dad?'

'Yes?'

'You know, before you can be hard . . . well, you have to give in, don't you? I mean, you have to be resigned, accept things and then harden yourself?'

'I suppose.'

'I can't do it. I don't accept.'

'Accept what?'

I couldn't answer him.

'Frances, you can't argue with death! He's gone! Holy God, that's a doomed rebellion if ever there was one!' We were quiet for a few moments.

'Maybe you've had it too easy,' he said. 'Never wanting for anything. What would you have done if you'd been me, eh? Beaten with a strap in school nearly every day! You know why? For getting things wrong, what do you think of that? Beaten for a spelling mistake or a wrong sum. And home wasn't any better. If I refused to eat my food any time, do you know what happened? Well?'

I shook my head.

'It was placed in front of me, unheated, at each meal until I ate every morsel. Imagine that, cold herrings or lumps of greasy stew put out at every meal, even breakfast, until I had to . . . I just had to . . .' His face turned red.

'A doomed rebellion,' I said. 'You gave in then you hardened yourself.'

'How else can anybody manage?'

' "Manage!" I don't want to simply endure things. Life should be wonderful!'

'God, you do sound like her.'

'There has to be more to it than toeing the line, paying the bills on time, holding your breath and hoping that nothing will crush you!'

'Paying the bills, don't make me laugh! I can't see how you're ever going to get into first gear as far as that's concerned! What sort of job are you going to get without qualifications?'

'I'll get a job.'

'Like hell you will! Listen to me, Frances, would you not apply for University again in the new year? Don't pull a face! You apply in January, right, you have until October to change your mind. Six months to revise for the exams. It would take your mind off . . . Will you do it? For my sake if not for your own?' The mirage of University resurrected itself before me. Intense debates, endless coffee, essay deadlines, the smell of books and polished corridors.

'OK.'

'That's the girl! There's no need to cry about it!'

'It's nothing. I just hate the thought of you being force-fed, that's all!'

'There, there, now! Never did me a pick of harm!' He backed out of the door before I could change my mind. I did not want to agree, only to be agreeable, for once, to my father.

I wanted to stay away from people, away from beliefs. I was afraid of violence, its constant threat and unalterable course. The retributive rage of people so obdurate in their hates and certainties. How could I defend myself against them? Unless I became the same? Became the sort of person I abhorred. I already knew about the apprentice hater inside me. Something else made me uneasy as well. Something boastful and self-important about living in a violent city. A perverse parochial conceit.

'*Yes, I was there. I witnessed that horror.*'

Accept, my father said. The death of one adult male. Plenty more where he came from. And the universe was not one atom more or less because of his death. A necessary sacrifice. The wheels of history revolving. Sins of the fathers. 'If your name's on it . . .'

Accept one death. Accept thousands.

To him such surrender would indicate mastery of the adult world.

Accept parental guidance, that was part of his message too.

Keep your head down. Follow the routes festooned with rewards.

Go to University and scoop up the qualifications, the status, the contacts. An entrance fee to a cushy job. So long as you keep faith with the taboos and niceties, the emblems and slogans of our little set. Our little sect.

To hell with knowledge, understanding, ideals. He was right about that. In a way. You had only to see the brainless sulky confidence on the faces of British soldiers. You had only to listen to the changeless battle cries of the Ulster Volunteer Force, the Ulster Freedom Fighters, the Ulster Defence Association, the Irish Republican Army, the Irish National Liberation Army . . . to realise that no amount of intellectual and moral critique had anything to do with those who sought their answers in blood. Measuring the abyss would not bring about its removal.

But I wept for my father's humiliation as a child, forced to eat repulsive food. Maybe that was why he loved to say: 'You'll eat your words one of these days!' His parents knew how to create a servant, not a man.

' "Do not go gentle into that good night" ', I murmured to myself. Suddenly I remembered one of my grandmother's concentration camp stories. There were certain prisoners who electrocuted themselves on the perimeter fences of the camps rather than walk into the gas chambers. They acted out of despair and terror, she said. But I knew there was pride in it too. A refusal. They chose the time and means of their deaths. Cheated their murderers. I would never give consent to Nick's death. Never consent to anything that ought not to be. Inevitable is only a word.

I began to study furiously for my examinations, spurred on by relief that Stella's own 'plan' to enter University had turned out to be a whim. I started to think about sex again. To feel sexual again. I dared not touch myself because of the half-formulated fear that God would punish me by killing off someone else that I loved. To placate Him, I tore up my only photograph of Nick. He began to disappear from my thoughts for long periods. Even from my dreams. Dying at last. Time was piling up its evidence: 'not here, not here.'

Autumn arrived. University. I chose to read Philosophy and Psychology, because they were new and unknown to me. I was glad that my former classmates were a year ahead. They ignored me and I was grateful. It made me grin to see that they still stuck together in their little cliques. I was determined to make new friends and chatted conscientiously to even the most unpromising neighbours in lecture halls, foisted myself on groups of students in the coffee bar. Not the animated purposeful ones who looked as if they were refuelling for the next bout of intellectual stimulus. I chose the pockets of resistance, the jaded witty malingering types who carried no books and rarely ventured outside the Students' Union.

My own studies were disappointing. Psychology focused on the measurement of intelligence and the training of rats to press levers. Philosophy was an arid lexicographical search. What do we mean by 'free', 'right', 'good', 'bad'? What do we mean by 'mean'? The lecturers were like diligent sleuths, accumulating and dispensing passionless detail. Soon I was one of the permanent dossers in the Union, talking politics, attending meeting after smoke-filled meeting.

That's how I fell in love with Paul Daly. He participated frequently in 'New Ireland' debates. A sarcastic rousing speaker. Sometimes his voice was a raw aggrieved . . . whine. Yes, he whined. And it upset me. It caused or reached some turbulence inside me.

At first I disliked Paul, so that even the sight of his name on a society poster irritated me. His face was gaunt and cruel, I thought, until I would see him again, and then those same facial contours seemed to denote sensitivity and grace. Which was the true interpretation? What is the meaning of 'true'?

He began to obsess me. I was always hoping to run into him. Planning to run into him. His girlfriend was Jessica Jacobs. My obsession included her. Sometimes I thought more about her than him. A tall redhead with fair almost translucent skin, a look of placid disdain on her features. Paul and Jessica. Always together. Their matching motorbike helmets resting side by side, their cigarette smoke forming one cloud. Often I stood outside after meetings watching them still exchanging jokes and jargon with their friends. Then they would mount the cycle and roar off to . . . . whatever they roared off to.

I must have him. I would never have him.

I had given up hope when the chance came. Near the end of

Michaelmas Term I was at a sparsely attended meeting. Paul came and sat beside me. No sign of Jessica. Suddenly this was the last thing I wanted! He kept glancing at me, muttering witty rejoinders to the speeches. I rose to leave.

'Hey, hang on for the vote!'

'I can't. I've got to get home early!'

'I'll leave you home.'

'No. No thanks. It's too far.'

'Where do you live, San Francisco?'

'Belmont.'

I saw him thinking 'Protestant'. 'Sure that's no bother. Sit yourself down.'

'What about a crash helmet?'

'What about it?'

'Well, it's the law . . .'

'Only for bikers.'

'Oh!'

'Relax. I've got a motor tonight. Leave you home in style.'

He was a tense skilful driver. His hands were beautiful. I kept looking from them to the outside, worried that Paul must be secretly sneering at the middle-class ease of my district. 'Rhododendria' was what he called it in speeches. The habitat of bankers, civil servants, and other parasites. Our talk was stiff and desultory. Too soon we reached my house. I couldn't get out of the car.

'The handle's down there,' he pointed.

'I want you to come in,' I said, catching my own imploring sounds.

He stared at me. 'To come in what?'

'Inside.'

'That's what I thought you meant!' He drew me towards him and kissed my mouth and neck. 'You should never look at a man like that!'

I was trembling.

'What's wrong?'

'No one's kissed me for long time.'

'Criminal neglect.'

'I love you.'

He released me abruptly. 'What's your name?'

'Frances McDowell. Fran for short.'

'But you're not, are you? You're a "forever" girl.' He spoke with hostility but then held and kissed me again with softness and longing.

123

He caught my hand as I slid it under his sweater.

'It's not a good idea! You'd better go!'

'I can't.'

He looked almost afraid. 'It's just sex, that's all!'

'Liar,' I whispered.

'Go away, go away now.'

He did not look back as he drove off.

Two days later I met him in the Library forecourt. I felt myself blush alarmingly. He was frowning. Suddenly we were in each other's arms.

'OK.' he kept saying. 'OK.'

We walked, holding each other like drunks, to his bedsitter and made love fiercely and too fast. Afterwards we lay slumped and speechless. The room was bleak and bare. A photograph of Jessica was pinned to the wall. Her silk scarf dangled from the doorknob. The phone rang in the corridor outside. Paul didn't move. He seemed to stop breathing. It must be Jessica, I thought. Who else would go on letting it ring with no reply? I imagined her swearing, exhaling her cigarette smoke sharply.

Silence.

'I can't see you again,' Paul told me. 'I'm not free.'

'You do a fair impersonation.'

He shook his head. 'What do you want of me?'

'Some time.'

'I'm getting married this Easter.'

I stood up. 'I won't bother you again.'

He was staring at my breasts.

'Would you mind turning away while I get dressed?'

'A bit late for shyness, isn't it?'

'Please.'

The term was over. A whole month without the hazard of seeing him. Or Jessica. I imagined them spending Christmas together, exchanging gifts, planning their marriage. He would be full of renewed penitential love. Perhaps he would even confide? A censored version probably. 'This wee slag . . . spoilt Prod brat thought she had only to crook her finger . . . threw herself at me . . . not a patch on you . . .' It would add fervour to their love-making.

I cried so much, it bored me. I made New Year resolutions. To bury myself in work. To disappear completely from Paul's sight. I knew I could do it. No Nick. No Paul.

On New Year's Eve my parents were preparing to go out to a posh dinner, when our doorbell rang.

'It's a bit early for the taxi,' my father grumbled as he went to answer the Intercom. 'It's someone for you, Fran. A Paul Daly.'

'Who?' said Stella, 'Oh, really, why didn't she say she'd invited some boyfriend round? So underhand. Suppose she thought we'd be out by the time he arrived!' I lifted the Intercom receiver.

'Hello?'

'Fran!'

'What do you want?'

'To talk to you.'

'I'm listening.'

'Let me see you!'

'What for?'

'I'll keep pressing the bell until you come outside!'

'Oh, all right.'

He was standing in the porch, soaked with rain.

'How did you get so wet?'

'Couldn't remember which house. I've been walking up and down . . . Well? Can I come in?'

I took his dripping scarf and coat that was warm inside with his body heat.

'There's a fire in here,' I said, ushering him into the dining room.

'God, what a fancy place! It makes me feel . . . shabby.'

'Then we're even, aren't we?'

His face was damp with rain or sweat. Even his teeth seemed to glisten in the subdued light.

'I've broken with Jessica.'

He was like a dog that had just dropped a dead bird at his owner's feet.

'So?'

'I did it for you! Because of you!'

'Nobody asked you!'

My mother appeared in the doorway, flashing her jewels and scanning Paul from head to foot. I could tell she liked the look of him despite his poor clothes.

'We're leaving now, Darling. Sorry we don't have time to get acquainted, Mr . . . ah . . . Are you Fran's latest beau? She never tells us anything!'

'I hope we will get acquainted, Mrs McDowell,' he said. He was still smiling when she left the room.

'Well, am I your latest beau? Am I?'

Suddenly it seemed a light and harmless thing to slide into his embrace.

Paul was married that Easter. To me. The brief ceremony took place in the Belfast registry office in the presence of two witnesses while another wedding party queued outside in the corridor. Both our families disapproved of our marriage and would not countenance a wedding in the 'other side's' church.

I told myself I was relieved not to have to glide down an aisle in an atavistic white uniform but perhaps it would have made me more 'married'. As it was, I felt involved in a mildly disreputable adventure, an interim phase.

Our parents' prejudice and spite did not bother me much. They made me feel romantically defiant. It was the resentment of Paul's friends that distressed me. They made no secret of their belief that Paul had committed an act of apostasy, a calculated move to enhance his future career by marrying into a well-connected Protestant family. The fact that my father had refused to attend the wedding and was barely civil to Paul cut no ice. But they did not shun Paul. Far from it. It was as if they set out to reclaim him by rarely leaving us alone. In my presence they loved to mention Jessica with a kind of militant nostalgia. 'Remember when you and Jessica . . . Jessica used to say . . . Saw Jessica the other day . . . looking great, so she was . . .'

It was even worse when they would suddenly start speaking Irish, as if I could not be trusted to hear certain things.

They regarded my Republicanism as an affectation, or perhaps an aberration. I became convinced that they felt more comfortable with hardline Protestant bigots, their own mirror images. The first quarrels between Paul and me were over his friends. He refused to notice their subtle persecutions and exclusions of me. 'It's you who's unfriendly and suspicious. They're not used to you, that's all.'

'Not used to me! They see me bloody often enough!' I felt more like a new unwelcome stepsister to the whole gang than a wife to Paul. Especially since Paul only wanted to make love rarely and perfunctorily. I could not understand it. How could passion extinguish itself so soon? Did the legitimization of sex through marriage kill the excitement? Did Paul feel shoddy because of Jessica or because of our families' hostility? Did I disappoint . . .? Did I disgust . . .?

I tried to talk to him. Formulated in my mind the question 'Why don't we make love more often?' But it always came out as 'Why don't you love me?'

Sometimes he reacted with furious irascibility, shouting and walking out; other times he insisted that he did love me, he loved me 'more than ever', so deeply that he felt at my mercy. He talked about his love as if it were some mysterious malignant tumour growing uncontrollably inside him.

My parents' attitude thawed and we were summoned occasionally for dinner. Stella always treated Paul like an ambassador from a foreign country. 'Tell me, what do the Catholics really want? Do Men desire offspring? Can Men be truly monogamous?' She would lean forward, watching him in a bemused flirtatious way as he gave his quiet patient answers. And I would watch her. She was like some island dweller starved of news. My parents were so safe and sure-footed in their mutual resentment they hardly noticed each other any more. Stella was still living solely for her weekly visits to the doctor's office, for that scheduled unilateral ration of intimacy. A despised husband, an adored therapist: her impotent jailors. And yet she was beautiful, intelligent. It seemed that sheer stupidity and wilful waste separated her from happiness. I must not let that happen to me out of pride and cowardice.

And so I tried harder with Paul. Too hard. I was so ardent and attentive! I could hear my own voice plucking at him. Begging.

Everything I did was wrong. When I brightened our flat with cushions and plants, he accused me of hankering for former comforts. When I criticized the Brits, the UDA, the IRA ('different armies, same brutality') I was a faint-hearted liberal. When I condemned the Brits' latest unprovoked shooting, I was ingratiating myself with his friends.

One day in the second year of our marriage Paul arrived home unexpectedly in the middle of the afternoon. It was odd because he had just started a job in the local hospital pathology laboratory after graduating in the summer. He felt sick, he said, and had walked out. I could smell drink on his breath.

'Liquid lunch?' I asked.

'No! Why do you always think it's my fault?'

'Keep your lid on. I'll make a pot of tea.'

But he said not to bother. Suddenly he approached me, pushed back the wings of hair from my face and stared. I tried to smile, but his eyes would not connect with me. Slowly, efficiently, he removed my clothes until I was naked.

'Love in the afternoon?' I joked.

He kept frowning and did not launch into any of the swift technicalities which he called foreplay. He cupped my breasts in his hands as if testing their weight, then circled me, surveying my body. He tweaked my waist and I started to tremble, waiting for his fingers to poke at me like cattleprods.

I turned round angrily, determined to make him look me in the face.

'Paul . . .'

'Don't swing your breasts like that.'

'What!'

'Cover yourself up.'

An exercise in humiliation. But why? And why did he discourage my sexual initiatives, forbid amorous gestures in public? He feared women, I decided eventually. It was intolerable that he should only fear me. I remembered his revulsion for his mother who had borne nine children. He was always criticizing her sagging exhausted flesh, her 'bovine' resignation. Yes, he was afraid of flesh, vulnerable appetite-ridden flesh, that reproduced itself, aged, sickened, died. He could not bear to witness the story of his own mortal weakness in another's body. This is what I told myself.

He became even more surly towards me. I worried obsessively about my marriage, about turning out like my mother, repeating her sorrows. But it occurred to me that Paul resembled her more than I did. The same unfathomable bitterness, those little jabs of severity and spite alternating unpredictably with bursts of tenderness and vitality. It was like moving house and finding the same old wallpaper, the familiar furniture. I tried to distance myself from him, dedicating myself to studying for Finals, joining a prisoners' support group and campaigning to win political status for the men and women on the 'dirt' protest.

Within the space of one fortnight two of Paul's colleagues were murdered. Sectarian killings. He was deeply shocked and grieved, but I did not suspect how much, until he overdosed on sleeping pills and ended up in a psychiatric ward.

The hospital doctor told me that the deaths of his friends had been a breaking point: the Troubles had been preying on his mind for a long time. It was a commonplace occurrence, he said. Whole areas of Belfast and Derry were floating in a cloud of Valium.

It was strange to visit Paul in that wretched ward. The distress of seeing him so ill was offset by his renewed gentleness towards me. 'Never leave me,' he would plead and clutch at my hands. He rambled incessantly about Ireland, how it had blighted our lives, how we must get away. A fresh start. It did not cheer me to hear this kind of talk. No one had ever looked or smelt less fresh than Paul. He did not have the vigour or optimism necessary for new beginnings, I thought. When Paul was released from hospital with a prescription for tranquillisers and sleeping pills, he refused to go back to work. In a couple of months, I would graduate and we would go to England.

'Whereabouts in England?' I would say.

'Anywhere.'

Sometimes when I looked at his dreaming eyes and the new straggly beard that put years on him, I wanted to caress and hold him, but he killed the temptation with a glance.

He was muzzy and weak all the time from the drugs. He decided to flush them down the toilet. His irritability returned full force. Everything I did annoyed him: the way I sat, my pronunciation of certain words, my habits. 'In sickness and in health,' I kept telling myself. If he caught me smoking, he would grab my wrist and make me extinguish the lit tobacco.

'Christ, it was easier to love you when you were doped!' I blurted out once.

He looked young and stricken. 'Don't you love me?'

'Yes. Yes.'

'You said you didn't!'

'I do! I was exasperated. You drive me crazy!' I was amazed to see him weep. I went to him. Sexual intercourse was resumed. It was grim and sporadic. I never felt that we were making love. I was nursing him.

'Pregnant?' His face turned sickly grey.

'Yes! Isn't it wild?' I laughed.

'This can't happen! How did it happen?'

'Shall I draw you a diagram?'

'It's you! You've not been taking your pills! That's right, isn't it? Isn't it?'

'What's the point of taking the damned pills when I live practically like a nun!'

'You flatter yourself . . . I can't have a child!'

I stood up. 'Well, that's all right, Paul. You're not the one who's going to.'

'Please, Fran.'

'Please what?'

'Get rid of it. No, come here. I'll never ask you to do anything for me again, I swear.'

'God, I don't believe this . . .'

'I can't be a . . .father.'

'You are a father. That's what you are. The baby's here, inside, growing inside me. God, what sort of Catholic are you, anyway? It's a mortal sin what you're saying. Asking me to kill a human soul.'

'A soul can't be killed.'

'No, but your soul would be damned eternally, wouldn't it? Isn't that a part of your superior creed?'

'I'm already damned! You know nothing! You see nothing!'

'I know that if you had any love for me . . .'

'I don't.'

'What did you say?'

'I don't love you. I can't love you.'

It was more like the foyer of a hotel than a clinic. A London clinic. Our first port of call in England. Starting our new life by ending one. The operation cost two hundred pounds of the money which my parents had given to tide us over the first few weeks. But babies are expensive, as everyone knows.

The receptionist led me into the surgery. Two doctors sat at the desk facing me. The younger one was flicking through holiday brochures: Thomson's, Sovereign, Cosmos. The other one looked over my case notes.

'Are you sure you want to go through with this?'

'Yes.'

I wondered if he would require some display of hysteria.

'Could you repeat your reasons?'

'It's an accidental pregnancy. My partner and I are looking for work. We have no suitable accommodation.'

'Right. Right,' he murmured.

He signed the form. So did the other one.

'Do I pay you?'

'No, no! The receptionist will handle that.'

In the anteroom to the theatre, I lay on a trolley and waited my turn. I closed my eyes and repeated over and over what I had read in the medical books: The foetus at seven weeks is half an inch long. Only half an inch.

*

'*C'est fini . . . Finito . . . Finito . . . C'est fini* . . . That one's Irish . . .
Oh, funny . . . Wake up, love . . . All over, dear. Come on . . .'

I dreamed of Nick. Was my baby with . . .? My hospital gown was
soaked when I woke again in the private room. I reached between my
thighs and withdrew my hand smeared with blood. 'The Red Hand of
Ulster', I thought, giggling stupidly.

'*That one's Irish.*'

No abortion in Northern Ireland, you see, I imagined explaining to
the nurses. Illegal, immoral, impossible. Only 'ex utero' human beings
may be killed there with impunity. An advanced civilisation.

But I was no better. An accomplice of death, after all. Paul came at
six. I had the initial shock of pleasure I always felt at the sight of him,
the line of his jaw, his dark hair.

'All right?' he said.

I nodded. I could not speak for a moment. If only he would do
something; show by some touch or word that he knew what I had done,
something might be salvaged between us.

'You can be free now,' I said. 'We can separate.'

'You're my wife.'

'What does that mean? Are only babies disposable?'

'I'm sorry,' he whispered.

'Too late.'

He took me back to rooms he had found in Notting Hill. He let me wail
like a wounded animal while he stroked and soothed me. A few days
later I had to start hunting for a job. Paul worked casually in bars. My
degree was an obstacle to finding work. I stopped mentioning it and
was offered a clerical job in an architects' firm. At weekends Paul and I
were tourists, visiting Speakers' Corner, the Tower, the Dungeon, the
galleries. He was remote but gentle. He seemed to be gentle.

Coming home one ordinary day to find him gone. Gaps on the
bookshelf, space in the wardrobe. The rooms neat as a surgical
operation.

His note on the pillow.

How did he decide which books were 'his' and which 'mine'? I
pictured him selecting, discarding, applying his terrifying justice to our
property.

Next day I discovered the things he left behind. Item: one camera, film unused. Item: one postcard: Piccadilly in the sunshine. Item: one old sweater.

His smell on the bedclothes. His silence in every room.

His silence.

15

Words
September 1984

Words. Love of words. Distrust of words. Holding them at bay while I check for poison. Beware especially of those words that block off the exits:

It's a girl!
I do!
Guilty!

President Reagan has christened the MX missile 'The Peacemaker'. 'You don't have to read that,' I told myself. 'You don't have to know.' Turn the pages. The Women's Page. 'That means me.'

Recipes written by a man, full of penny-pinching, ecologically sound advice. 'Soup or stock can be made out of almost anything. Cauliflower stalks and leaves, vegetable peelings, even potato skins, but be sure to scrub off the dirt first.'

'No thanks,' I told him. 'I know all that, how to scrimp and save, make soup out of garbage, make do and mend, make ends meet, make love not war, make men mad . . .' Article on pregnancy and poverty, a survey showing that Hackney mothers are less well nourished than Hampstead mothers and their babies suffer as a result. Surprise surprise.

The main article, an interview with a zoo owner who prefers animals to people. Can't wait for the nuclear holocaust to wipe out the blemish of humanity. If my daughter were being attacked by one of my tigers, he declares, I would save the tiger.

'The Peacemaker.' It kept coming to the surface of my mind. The MX missile guarding our peace, *creating* our peace. Bringing you the peace of the cemetery at the flick of a switch. The peacemakers with their prisons, their police, their pills, their greedy pyres. Heinrich Himmler stared into the burial pit, where people were forced to lie down naked on top of the freshly dead to be shot. He had never seen a corpse before and he couldn't get enough of it. Until his face got splattered with some exploding brain and he ran away to vomit. Later, pale and shaken, he called his merry men together. 'I cannot spare you this,' he told them. 'I cannot spare you.' A merciful man who knew his duty. Who lit his darkness with lamps shaded with human skin. Consoling constant evidence of the death of the 'enemy'. Words cannot be trusted. They are the lipstick on the corpse. The fake grass covering the snakepit.

An advertisement on television. Close-up of two timepieces, a man's watch, big and square, a woman's watch, dainty and pretty. 'These are the true faces of love,' the voice says.

The rapist denies his act. 'I couldn't make love to her,' he confesses. She was beaten, tied down. His friends took it in turn to 'make love' to her. But he could not 'make love' to her. No one protests at this use of language.

The child giggles, thinking it must be a game. They lay her lovingly on the ground. Her mother holds down her arms. Her grandmother and the new lady spread her legs. Slicing begins. Screaming begins. First the clitoris. Then the lips, inner and outer. They tug the severed folds of skin together and sew them up to cover the urethra and the vaginal entrance. If she dies, they will bury her secretly. If she lives, they will say she is healed. No one questions this use of language.

I hate 'love'. Love won horizontally. Love spread thick and thin. Love set to music. Sateen hearts and plastic flowers. Love, love me, do . . .You know I love you. Love me, you fuckers . . .

Love is a word that should be earned.

Here's a story. This story never happened but it's true.

The girl and the tiger are in the fenced enclosure. The girl brings fresh water. She speaks gently to the tiger, who paces back and forth, back and forth, sometimes pawing at flies in the air.

The man approaches, smiling. He is the owner. He owns the girl, who is his daughter.

He owns the land, which stretches as far as the eye wants to see.

He owns the tiger. But she does not understand possession.

The man loves the tiger. More than people, more than his child, more than himself. But she does not understand comparison.

He loves her for what she can do. Run for miles at astonishing speed, spring on her prey in controlled graceful leaps, survive by her cunning and her strength.

He does not allow her to do these things.

He kneels beside her, stroking her fur, feeling her warm breath on his face. 'My beauty,' he whispers.

She does not understand his language. She eats him.

And here's a love story. A true love story.

Sometimes tears started in the woman's eyes as she saw the changes in her daughter's body. Her face was becoming gaunt. Collar bones and elbows painfully exposed. Breasts flattened. She was skin and bone. Embraces hurt her. Once the mother could not stop herself, and she cried out: 'These should be your most beautiful years!'

But quickly she added: 'We will survive! I know we will survive!' She said it every day, no tremor in her voice, no doubt.

It was five weeks before the liberation. Food was scarcer and scarcer.

They were dying by inches.

A fellow prisoner was pregnant, approaching the time of birth. They watched over her with hope and dread, the mismatch of her poor skeletal frame and the life-filled belly. Everywhere the stench of rotting bodies, but the baby kept on growing, preparing itself. It was like a tiny shake of the fist.

The birth pangs came and the woman was dragged off into the operating room. Her friends heard her screams, and like so many times before, they had to muzzle their own mouths with their fists, they had to conquer themselves. At last the SS soldier emerged carrying the baby. He marched to the sink, filled it with water, and dunked the baby's head.

'Goodbye, little Moses.' Strange, almost tender voice. A benediction, 'Goodbye, little Moses.' Did he say it to taunt and torment the women? Or, even in his tireless campaign against life, did he hesitate to kill the baby fresh from the womb, born in such agony, against such odds? Did he have to remind himself that the child belonged to the odious expendable race before he could murder him? The baby is dead, in any case.

One day the daughter managed to get a bowl of soup. A miracle! She carried it to her mother, careful to spill no drop, but walking swift and stealthily, afraid that someone would pounce at any moment and steal the food.

'Look, Mama! Look what I have!'

'O my darling! Eat! Eat!'

'It's for you!'

'I cannot. Please . . . You are young. Please. It was my prayer.'

The girl held out the bowl. 'Here.'

135

The mother shook her head.

These refusals went on for some time.

'I know,' the daughter proposed. 'One spoonful each, in turn.'

The mother agreed. Each woman took tiny sips, letting most of the soup dribble back into the bowl.

'We'll get nowhere like this!' the mother laughed. 'Let's feed each other.'

And so, in turn, each woman filled the spoon to brimming and held it to the other's mouth. They were both mother and child, nurturer and receiver.

A few days later, the Allies arrived. That chance bowl of soup may have saved the women's lives.

After the liberation, there were survivors who sought revenge on German civilians. Once the daughter witnessed such an attack, a young German woman with a small baby surrounded by a raging crowd brandishing sticks. The girl remembered Moses. 'No, no,' she screamed. She ran to a passerby. 'They're going to kill the baby! No more babies must die!' They rushed over to the crowd. The wrath of the mothers rose in her, the screams of the silenced hearts.

'No more babies!' she shrieked. 'No more babies! No more babies!' Everyone stopped. Gradually, the people started to move off. The mother took to her heels, carrying the baby, abandoning the pram.

The man took the girl in his arms. 'My dear, after what you have suffered, how have you preserved so much love?'

'I didn't preserve love,' she answered. 'Love preserved me.'

16

Doing Time

Speak! Speak! Speak!

I had woken up looking straight at the girl, whose face registered no emotion. As usual! The silent watcher. Perhaps she never slept? Just lay there all night listening to the banging and screams from other cells, some distant, some near, the prison's night music. It shouldn't have bothered me, I thought. Most nights at Greenham the soldiers kept up a stream of sexual abuse and threat. But it's easier to listen to cries of hatred than of anguish, I discovered. In here those sounds of desolation and hopeless insurrection had driven me one night to start banging on the door hatch myself, shouting and begging for silence. After that I asked for a nightly sedative, although I hated the thought of numbing my senses. Even with medication, my sleep remained shallow, nervy, infiltrated by *her* presence. Maybe I talked at night? Was that why she hated me? I was sure that she hated me. My dreams were vivid and frightening, more like memories, really. I had named and researched my terrors: nuclear war, nuclear winter, universal death. Sleeping or awake, I had the same nightmare.

During the long lonely daytimes, I relived the trial at Newbury Court. Seven of us charged with breaching the peace and damaging property for cutting the perimeter fence to enter the base. Speech after eloquent speech from the women. Powerful and distressing evidence about the Genocide Act, the Geneva Convention, the vulnerability of the base (if we could get in, anybody could!). Time after time, we challenged the magistrates: 'We cannot be silenced.'

'I cannot be bound over. I am keeping the peace. I ask you to keep it.'

'We are not on trial. You are.'

'I'm on trial for my life. And my children's lives.'

'Have you children?'

It was the faces of the magistrates that terrified me. They looked alike. They showed no human emotion, except for occasional mild irascibility. Might as well plead with stones. Our motives were irrelevant. The threat to humanity was irrelevant. They were determined to stick-to-protocol and do-their-duty.

I could imagine them post-Holocaust. Smooth grey men in smooth grey suits, beavering away in their municipal bunker, updating their index cards and computer records with tallies of the dead and dying. They would carry out the job mechanically, irritably, perfectly, just like any other administrative task.

The sleek shall inherit the earth. The dearth.

We were sentenced to fourteen days each, taken from the court to the waiting 'meatwagon' and locked into the tiny wired cubicles. How sick I was of looking at wire! During the long journey to London, my head cracked twice against the metal wall. Kathy kept complaining about nausea. Finally she started to moan and then vomited. I closed my eyes, yearning to reach Holloway!

Warmth, food, rest, shelter, company! A real bed under a real roof!

But Holloway was pure hell. Three prison warders processed us through the admissions ritual. A strict motherly woman with a 'down-to-business' face. An aging Sindy Doll heavily made up and doused in scent. She looked as if she had put on the uniform for a joke. A nervous young woman with the appeasing voice of inexperience. She kept looking back and forth from prisoners to colleagues, hoping to earn the approval of both. In a separate room I had to strip naked and hand over my clothes for searching. Then I had to bend over while Sindy investigated my anus.

'I am not a criminal,' I kept thinking. 'I cannot be ashamed.'

But I was. How easy it is to be humiliated through the body! I thought about the Nazis and their systematic degradation of the Jews. A trick every oppressor knows, how to activate the victim's self-loathing.

When I stood up again, it was as if I were not naked. I stared directly at the senior officer. She gave a little pout of indignation before her face blanked again. I had forgotten that all women are not sisters.

Do you know what the government plans for us after the Bomb? I asked them silently. The survivors will be divided into 'co-operative' and 'criminal'. Co-operative survivors. Criminal survivors. Even after the Bomb, the enemy will not be dead.

I was isolated from the other campaigners. We were all deliberately split up, we found out later, because previous groups of Greenham women had been a 'disruptive influence', refusing to work and being generally subversive.

I was allocated to a room already occupied by a young black woman with short smooth hair like a sheared lamb. Her eyes were quenched: they belonged to someone older.

It is very demoralising to talk to somebody who does not respond. My chatter began to sound too loud and falsely cheerful before it dwindled and stopped. Time started to slow down. Confinement in that small cell with this ominously withdrawn woman was torture. I had no books with me, no writing paper. I was too wound up to sleep. Nothing to do but wait: the main 'activity' in prison. Waiting for meals, waiting for exercise, waiting for visits, waiting for sleep, waiting for release. Weighting.

I was ravenous by the time dinner was served. But the food was inedible. Cold muck. When I was let out for 'association' (the other woman stayed in the cell), I thought that at least some conversation might distract me from my hunger. As I entered the long room, I saw a group of fellow prisoners alongside the wall. A large white woman gave me a surly glance. She looked like a store detective, I thought. The others reminded me of a group of unemployed disgruntled men at a street corner. They had the air of 'dying for something to happen.'

'Hey, it's one of them political prisoners!' There was a tinge of friendliness in the voice, softening the jibe.

'We're all political prisoners!' A thin serious woman.

'Got any cigarettes, Idealist?' the first one asked.

'Real ones, she means,' someone else said eagerly. 'Not roll-ups.'

'Sorry, I don't smoke.' I blushed, embarrassed that I had nothing to offer them.

'Is there any way of getting some food round here?' I asked quickly. 'Like chocolate?'

They laughed delightedly. 'You should take up smoking! Gets your mind off the food. Better for your health, too!'

'It wouldn't surprise me. But after tonight's dinner, surely it can only get better?'

'Don't you kid yourself, love. Sometimes there's even slugs in that garbage they expect us to eat!'

'No! I don't believe you!'

Silence. A circle of reproving eyes.

'You sound just like a screw, Miss!'

'Sorry. I didn't mean . . . it's just an expression . . .'

139

'Listen, you, a woman in here died from that food. They snuck her out, took her to Styal in the middle of the night, said she was killed by some mystery bug. But we reckon it was food poisoning.'

'And if you don't believe that, just you wait a while. By the time you walk out of here, you'll believe it all right and plenty more!'

'I have heard . . . things. Some of the women at the camp who've been here told me about the headbashing that goes on in the 'disturbed' wing. And about the girl who burned to death in her cell while two screws went to ask someone in charge what to do!'

'Yeah, it's a disgrace, that Muppet House!'

'Shame on you, Diana!' The rebuke came from a tall black woman who had not spoken before. 'That's a cruel name. Show some respect for those poor creatures that shouldn't be in jail at all. The Lord forgive you!'

'Oh, Arlene, everybody calls it the Muppet House! Why pick on me?'

'Right. Everybody calls it that. Including the screws. You can sink to their level if you want!' At that moment I was glad to see Jo arriving with Kathy, now recovered from her earlier sickness. Jo was good at entering rooms and getting acquainted with strangers. Perhaps because she regarded no one as a stranger. The women warmed to her at once and soon we were all sitting down together. Ignoring the screws, they talked first about the hardships of prison, the penalties and petty rules. Then Arlene began to talk about herself. A single parent with four small children. To feed them, she stole from shops, only the very best produce, steak and asparagus, shrimps, melons.

'Why should I stint my kids just cos their daddy don't care? Like it says in the Bible, if my son asks for bread, shall I give him a stone? If he asks for a fish, shall I give him a serpent? They can call me a thief, an *incorrigible* thief, if you please, but nobody can call me a bad mother!'

Diana started to weep softly at the mention of children. Hers were in care while she served her sentence. Her 'boyfriend' who had persuaded her to go on the game and lived off the earnings, had not been once to visit her in prison.

'He'll come round when you're due to get out, see if I'm wrong! Buttering you up and promising you the moon . . . Just don't let him get his hooks into you again!'

'Or anything else for that matter!' someone laughed. Diana wiped her eyes, mustered a smile. 'No. Never again. I've listened to him too many times.'

More stories spilled round the table. The women's crimes were mostly trivial, prompted by poverty and need. Petty theft, prostitution, possession of drugs, 'drunk and disorderly' charges . . . Many of them were bringing up children unaided, struggling to survive with all the resilience and nerve they could summon. Others were trapped by their dependence on drugs and alcohol, the need to curtail a reality that offered little hope.

Soon it was time for lockup. Just before I left, I whispered to Arlene about my cellmate.

'Oh, you're in with Marilyn.'

'What's wrong with her?'

'Nothing.'

'But she won't speak!'

Arlene gave the almost imperceptible shrug which I already recognised as the prisoners' most common gesture.

'She speaks when she decides. But I admit it's not exactly a habit! Look, don't you hassle her. Don't show her any dislike. That poor child's been in nothing but institutions all her life. Nobody wanted her. Foster families kept sending her back because she was trouble. And then there was a couple who wanted to adopt her but that didn't work out. They changed her name. "Marilyn" wasn't classy enough for them, so they fixed on Isabel. A little girl with nothing and they even take her name away! What's a five year-old child to make of something like that? It must have made her think "Marilyn" was all wrong and when they sent her back to the Home, it was cos she couldn't get that "Marilyn" badness out of herself. You see, darlin', for some people words is just something for getting hated in.'

Back in the cell, Marilyn was sitting on her bed, picking at her nails. She did not look up when I entered, but her face tautened. It was her only acknowledgement of me.

Next day, the same button-lipped routine. The window was in 'her' half of the cell and I did not dare go and look out of it. It was as if we could both see a line marking off her space and I could not violate it. I felt like a Yedizi tribeswoman caught inside a chalk circle. Each time I was let out of the cell I felt immensely thankful, even if I was ordered to scrub floors. At least I could talk to people and those brief simple moments of companionship were like rain in the desert.

In desperation to relieve my boredom, I asked a screw if I could borrow books from the Library. She told me that I would have to put in an application to the Governor. Permission would depend on the

Library Officer being available, enough other women being interested in going to justify an escorting officer, and an officer being free to accompany us. Unlikely in the current staff shortage situation.

'I've changed my mind,' I told her.

During the next few days . . . What an easy misleading phrase for those eternities! Nothing to do but watch my thoughts turn over. I was sinking fast without the rafts of constant activity and companionship. And I had imagined myself so much stronger.

At Greenham the constant evictions had at first defeated me. Even living in those privations, I saw how swiftly and naturally people grow attached to a particular site, to small belongings and arrangements, little anchors in chaos. Nothing could be more demoralising than to be constantly moved on, to watch the heartless destruction of equipment and property in the 'scruncher'.

But the more it happened, the stronger we became. I remembered Jo cheering us once by reading the words of a concentration camp survivor, Zdena Berger:

'You don't need walls and doors . . . Freedom is not a place you can own . . . It's a home inside yourself.'

But now for the first time in months, I worried about the future, my *personal* future, how I would manage with Emily. How I would survive economically and how I would cope with the stares and the prejudice. A white woman with a black child. I felt guilty for bringing Emily into a world that would not prize her. I felt guilty for feeling guilty. I wondered if my father would give me money if he knew my plight? Or would he disown me? My last contact with him was three Christmases ago. It was just after Stella's death and I thought that we should be together. I remember sitting up all night on the crowded ferry listening to carousals, snores, vomiting. It seemed an unfitting pilgrimage to the immaculate sterile house. My father, pale and haggard, his chin the only unclenched part of his face.

'Any men in your life?' It was his only question. Wanting to see me 'safely' married.

Any men in your life?

Dozens, Daddy.

The policeman who held my face down in the mud.

The soldiers who rolled my friends in barbed wire, while one who was eyeing them coldly, unzipped himself, yanked his thing and spurted immediately. No, I know, that's not what you meant.

I found myself praying constantly. To God the Father, God the Son,

God the Holy Ghost. The Old Triumvirate. Even though I despised Christianity. '*Unus Deus, Sancta Trinitas, Fili, Redemptor Mundi*,' I would whisper. Maybe it was a way of getting strong, entering a cool meditative state.

Dear Goddess, I experimented. Demeter. Diana. Athene. The Spinner. The spider's web. My hand flew to my face as I remembered the tracery of spider veins which had broken out over my cheeks in the icy conditions at the camp. My appearance had begun to distress me unutterably. Ruined manbait, I told myself. The physical exterior aspect of a person is the least important, ha-ha. I am not my body, ha-ha.

Dear Mother. Oh no, keep out of my mind. She died of a cerebral haemorrhage. A tiny explosion in the brain. Aneurysm. Basilar artery. I repeated the clinical terms to myself to try and banish the image of that welling of blood.

Marilyn started one of her coughing fits. Part of her wordless warfare, I was convinced. I turned my body to the wall. I longed to be alone. If I could be alone, I would . . . Walk up and down. Stare out of the window. Speak aloud. Sing to myself. Weep. Touch myself, my breasts, my stomach. Masturbate. Sleep deeply, properly. Dream freely.

At the camp I could wander off into the trees, lean against a trunk until I could bear to be with the others again. I moved my face closer to the wall. My face is alone, I thought. I reached underneath my jumper to hold my breasts which were always cool even when the rest of me was hot and uncomfortable.

Her racking cough again.

I leapt to my feet, glaring at her: 'I bloody wish I wasn't here too!'

No surprise, no reaction. Game, set, and match!

Later, Jo advised me to ask for a transfer to another cell. 'They've put you in with her deliberately, don't you see? It's their idea of humour.'

'I'd better stick it out.'

'Why?'

'I can't . . . she's goading me . . . She wants me to reject her. So I won't.'

There was more to it. I kept fantasising that Marilyn knew me instinctively, read my thoughts. That we were somehow connected. I thought that I understood her malignant loneliness, her desire to relinquish the world.

On the first Saturday, I started to speak. 'I'm going to talk. You can stop me if you like. Just say the word.'

I told her about things the other women had said, little incidents and jokes and gossip. Then about some of the women themselves, how I felt about each of them, about the prison, the camp, how we lived, then about myself, Emily . . . on and on with desperate candour, revealing more and more personal things. At first I felt good about it: I was not allowing her silence to gag me. But then I thought I was probably only fuelling her malice. All the bits of my past that I was carefully leaving out: Nick, Paul, Stella, started pressing in on me, and I felt my anger mounting, an anger not really connected with Marilyn, but with all those others who were beyond my reach. Misery rose in me like a physical pain and I shut up. Marilyn belched flamboyantly.

'Talk to me, you stupid cow!' I shrieked.

She gave me a calm scrutinizing stare. 'Ten minutes for your face cream,' she said.

'What?'

'You heard. You can have ten minutes if you hand over your face cream.'

'But I need . . . we could share it.'

'No.'

Slowly I fetched the cream, almost wanting to laugh and back out. I had imagined this moment of speech. The words were packed in Marilyn's mouth. Her lips would part. The room would explode in hot lava.

What a clown I was: the only interesting thing about me was my skin cream!

She took the jar and placed it under her pillow.

'Right, start.'

'I'm Fran. I know your name is Marilyn.'

'I know that too.'

'Well, how long have you been here?'

'Long enough.'

'Why don't you like to speak?'

'Who says I don't like to speak?'

'Why don't you speak?'

'There's no law that says I have to!'

'Why are you in here?'

'Got caught.'

'Where are you from?'

'Disneyland.'

'Give me back my cream!'

'I'm talking, aren't I?'

'But you won't say anything!'

'I'm from Hammersmith. And now ask me where I'm *really* from! Go on!'

'What do you mean?'

'Where are you really from? That's what they always say. As if I don't belong in this country.'

'People do that to me too. Because I'm Irish.'

'That doesn't make us mates. Next question.'

'Why are you in here?'

'Want to hear the real reason or the official excuse?'

'Both.'

'Non-payment of fine for soliciting, and assaulting a police officer. That was after he twisted my arm and called me coon-cunt but you're supposed to say thank you when they do that! The real reason . . . where do we start? "Trouble" is my middle name, that's what the social worker says. The case against me seems to be I'm black, fat, insolent, wilfully deaf, feckless, reckless, no-husband, no-pretty-please, no-civil-tongue-in-'er-'ead, can't-pay-for-nothing. Oh, did I leave out immoral? Immoral with persons of no social standing. That enough for you, is it?'

'Why do you keep all that anger bottled up inside you?'

'I don't! That's why I keep getting clobbered! Oh, fuck all this chitchat. Nothing but questions and interfering and nosiness!'

'You could ask me something.'

'Ask you something! You kidding? After the way you've been plaguing me with your life story! Know so much about you, I feel as if I was forced to sniff your knickers. I don't want to talk to you! Why should I pass your time for you, Daytripper? Be out of here in another week. Back up to bloody Berkshire to make collages out of your Tampax . . . Leaving that poor little baby behind, not giving it a second thought.'

'I look after her every other week. And when I'm not there, she's well cared for by other women!'

'They white?'

'Yes.'

'You're keeping that child away from her own people!'

'I'm her people.'

145

'I know how whites treat black kids. Like pet mongrel dogs. What age is she?'

'Nearly two.'

'Oh, well, high time she fended for herself!'

'Look, I have to leave her sometimes in order to look after her, don't you understand? To look after her future, while my friends look after her present!' She caught the note of hysteria in my voice.

'You've nearly run out of time. So get this. The reason why I don't say nothing for free is I'm sick of your kind. Here today, gone tomorrow, but you think you can amuse yourself poking your fingers through the bars of my cage, well you can't! Another thing, you thought you was smart saying: "I, Miss High and Mighty am going to talk to you, nothing you can do about it . . ." '

'I didn't say that.'

'Don't interrupt. You're lucky I didn't stop you with this!' She showed me her fist. 'And finally, I would just like to inform you that you get on my nerves. Why don't you ever keep still? Walking this way, walking that, it pains my eyes! Twisting your hair, hugging yourself, sighing all the while, moaning in your sleep like you're coming or something . . .'

'Christ! You get on my nerves too . . .'

'Time's up!'

Next day I played incommunicado too. A supporter came at visiting time with gifts for me and the other peace women. I took the precious hoard back to the cell. Freesias, a novel, a box of chocolates. I became engrossed in the book at once and kept trying to slow down my reading, make it last. Suddenly, Marilyn spoke making me jump.

'You could have a half-hour for those chocolates.'

'They're not for sale. Besides your conversation isn't worth it!'

I could not settle down to reading again. Arlene's words kept returning to my mind. I rose from the bed and threw the box, which landed on Marilyn's bed.

'You can have them for nothing.'

Her face lightened for a second, turned grim again.

'No. It has to be a proper swap. Otherwise I'll be beholden.'

'As you like. But I'll save up my half-hour till later.'

She kept stealing anxious glances at me. She hated being on a string, having an obligation to dispense. I made her wait till after supper.

'OK. Let's talk.'

'Right. You start.'

'No. You said you hate questions.'

'But just get us going.'

'Do you live alone?'

'Yes. Why? What's wrong with that?'

'Nothing. Have you a boyfriend?'

She smirked. 'Male and female created He them!'

'Any children?'

She started twisting the ring round her little finger. 'Yes and no.'

'What does that mean?'

'I have a little boy.'

'Got a picture?'

'A picture is all I've got.'

'Oh is he . . .?'

'Dead? No. They took him off me. I'm an unfit mother.'

'I don't believe that.'

'Course you don't. You think women shit pure caramel. Can't do wrong. Going to save the fuckin' world with their holiness.'

I ignored this, too tired to try and explain my 'philosophy'.

'I know now why you were so hard on me about Emily. You miss your own child so much, don't you?'

Her whole face twitched.

'I know how you feel . . .' I said.

She stood up. 'Don't you dare! Don't you dare say that! You want to sit in a wet field playing at survival, that's your choice! Hurting yourself is your little pass-time! Nobody forces you to do without your kid for one minute. You and your fuckin' team of do-good babysitters!'

'You can make fun of my lifestyle if you want . . .'

' "Lifestyle!" *Life-style!* She whooped.

'But if you'd shared mothering with other people, maybe you wouldn't have lost your son!'

Sobbing broke out of her without warning, deep racking sounds like crazed laughter.

'I didn't mean to . . .'

She was pacing about blindly, her arms shielding her chest.

'Please. I'm sorry.'

She calmed down at last, wiped her nose. 'Where you going?' she challenged when I rose from her bed.

I pointed to my side of the cell.

'Stay put! Going to tell you something, girl. About my Lifestyle! Turn your face away. No, sit with your back to me!'

'OK.'

'I was having a real hard time, never enough money. Lived in Clapham, just me and Jimmy. He was two. The flat was damp, horrible. Jimmy was never without a cold, always snuffling, never well. They were threatening to cut off my electric one time. Had to get money quick. I started slipping out at night to get it. Had to leave Jimmy on his own. I'm not a whore, I want you to realize. I only do it when it's strictly necessary. I hate doing it. Because I'm black, men think they can be primitive and uncouth with me. It's like I'm supposed to take their filth into me and neutralize it or something. Like some kind of garbage-eater . . . 'Anyway, that's off the point . . .' She was quiet for a few minutes, then resumed. 'This particular night, I was working cars. Some bastard comes along and drives me to the Common. When the business is done, he refuses to take me back, says "Take your bus fare out of what I give you." By the time I walk home, the police are all over the place, no sign of Jimmy. The room stinks. The police start their questions. Where was I? Am I the mother of . . .? Do I often leave him unattended? Am I on drugs? On and on till I'm nearly out of my head with not knowing where Jimmy is. Finally they tell me he's in hospital. With burns. I left an eleric bar heater on top of the sideboard before I went out. I thought it would be safe so high up! Well, I couldn't leave him with no warmth, could I?

'He must have woken up and started moving around. The orange light glowing in the dark would have attracted him, I suppose. He yanked the flex and the fire fell on him, on to his legs where it burnt and stuck. The guard must have come loose as the thing toppled. Jimmy would have died if the landlady hadn't heard him screeching. Second degree burns. That's what the smell was. Charred flesh. I was done for child neglect. I didn't fight to keep him. I thought I was bad for him. I *was* bad for him! The joke is, I always hated my mother for putting me in care, always swore I'd never let go of any kid of mine! You can turn round now. What are you crying for? I don't want your big crocodile tears. If you were the judge, you'd have taken him away from me, wouldn't you?'

'I'm not condemning you, Marilyn. I know the odds are piled against you . . .'

'Who said you could use my name?'

Next morning I came back from the toilet to find her looking at my half-read book.

'*The Color Purple*,' she read out the title dismissively. 'What's it about, anyway?'

'About a girl who's raped by her father. Her two kids are taken away from her and then she's married off to a widower who wants her to look after his children.'

'I see. A comedy.'

'It's actually a very joyous book.'

'Is it, *actually*?'

'Shall I read you some?'

'Up to you.'

'OK. Here's a bit where two women are talking about how useless their men are in bed: "I don't like to go to bed with him no more, she say. Used to be when he touch me I'd go all out my head . . ." '

She snatched the book. 'That's not how an American black woman speaks, you! Listen . . . I'll do it. Here, find me the place where the babies are taken away.'

She read it with a beautiful confidence, capturing the cadences exactly. After several episodes, she set down the book and said:

'She went through all that shit and it all came right in the end.'

'Yes.'

I watched her face harden again. She was protecting herself against hope. 'That's because it's a made up story,' she said finally.

It was the last day before my release. The prospect of getting out filled me with a strange dread. The new friends I had made were already distancing themselves. I realised it was their defence against the hurt of so many goodbyes.

My vision started to go haywire, objects dimming then erupting into prominence until finally I rushed to the toilet cubicle to vomit. I came back and curled up on the bed. Marilyn padded over.

'You sick or what?' she said gruffly.

I could not answer.

'Try and sleep.'

'Yes, sleep.'

I could not. There was a knifing pain behind my eyes. Suddenly Marilyn was peering at me, her face disjointed like a painting by Picasso.

'What a racket you're creating! Trying to make your last night one to remember, are you?'

'Migraine,' I whispered.

'You do look bad.'

I must have turned to lie on my side because I could no longer feel my tears.

'I'll call for the doctor.'

'No!'

I knew that she could get into trouble for doing so, that she would have to make a statement.

'Marilyn,' I whispered. She leaned close to me. 'I don't want to be moved to the hospital wing. I don't want to be alone.'

'No . . . Neither do I,' she said.

She sat down on my bed and placed her miraculously cold hand on my brow.

'Listen, you, you're doing everything wrong. You've got to lie still as the dead to stop it hurting. No more tossing and groaning . . . Quiet now. Don't move a muscle.'

She massaged my neck and shoulders until I drifted into sleep. Some time later I wakened. She was still there.

'Better?' she asked.

I shifted my head experimentally. 'It still hurts, but I can see properly. It's not so bad. O God, it's tomorrow already . . .'

'Move over.' She lay down beside me.

'Don't think about anything nasty. Let's forget about being in prison. Pretend we're in the Ritz. Oh no, that might upset your rich-girl conscience,' she laughed. 'Pretend we're sleeping out under the stars. In summer. All those stars, all those light years away. All light years out there, no heavy years . . . You're just scared. That happens to me too. Every time I come in here I think I'll go crazy. But hell really starts when I get out again. With my carrier bag and my forty quid discharge grant and nowhere to go except some rotten hostel. But full of big ideas! This time I will get a job, find a nice place to live, make friends, stay off drink and dope, be a good girl and even maybe be allowed to get Jimmy back. Sunday is the real killer. Lord's Day. Devil's Day, more like. Makes you remember everything you haven't got. Makes you count all your faults. No use trying to get away from it, everywhere you go there's that same sad empty look about things . . . But it'll be different for you, girl! Better get back fast to that Common before they start the Apocalypse without you!'

'Sometimes every day feels like Sunday,' I said.

'Yes, you know about that, don't you? You've got the look.'

'What look?'

'The "bad news" look.'

'What will happen, Marilyn?'

'Haven't got my crystal ball handy!'

'What will happen? To us, to everybody?'

'Out of our hands, girl. It's not our world.'

'Yes, it is,' I whispered and we fell silent.

Soon she was asleep and I started to shiver with fear and surprise because she had been so unrewardably good to me! All her rancour and archness had disappeared. And I had despised her barter system but perhaps I too had felt safer within its strictures.

Next morning someone hammered on the door at five o'clock.

'Get up McDowell, get ready for discharge!'

I knew I would have to face a formal procedure, another strip search. The final ordeal. I busied myself with washing, tidying up. Marilyn was wide awake, but studiously cool and remote as if she had already excised me from her mind.

'I'll come and see you, Marilyn,' I said just before leaving.

'Already have a social worker.'

'Don't be mean.'

'It won't do you any good, you know, fraternising with criminals!'

'Being locked up doesn't make you a criminal.'

'Yeah, and being killed don't make you dead.'

'I'll miss you.'

'Wish you'd hurry up and go!' she shouted.

'Is there anything you'd like me to bring you?'

She grinned suddenly: 'Better ring first before you drop by. In case I'm out shopping or something!'

17

Strangers

I was longing for a drink of water. A tall glass of fizzy mineral water with a slice of lemon. A blast of wind blew smoke towards us and Jo's eyes narrowed into a parody of a sexually knowing look, incongruous in her pinched cold face like a wink at a funeral. Coachloads of demonstrators had been arriving all morning. The air was filled with energy and bright greetings. Our dwindling stocks were being replenished with gifts of wood, fruit, home-baked bread.

'Look,' said Jo, 'more fire lighters. And here's another four litres of orange juice! Stick them with the rest of the lorryload. Reminds me of my wedding presents: six toasters and three percolators!'

'Jo? What do I look like?'

'The Avon lady.'

Laughing made me ache. It activated muscles best left numb.

'No, but really?'

'A refugee. Grimy but with a certain noble pathos.'

'Ugly, you mean.'

'Why don't you go and look in the mirror?'

'It broke. Yesterday. Or the day before.'

'Does that mean we'll live seven more years?'

Suddenly I had to get away from the smell of damp blankets and the sense of ramshackle festivity brought by the influx of visitors. I felt like part of a beleaguered exhausted troop at the sight of a rescuing cavalry.

'I'm going to walk about and get my circulation moving.'

'OK. Tea'll be ready in fifteen minutes if you're interested.'

'I wish I was home, home, home,' I thought as I trudged along, but the home in my mind was not one I had ever known. It was more like something out of an Ovaltine commercial, all rustic charm and fireside cosiness, cats and dogs, tea and biscuits, a clock ticking noisily as if to persuade that all moments are of equal duration.

'Better leave here soon,' I heard myself thinking for the thousandth time. The idea of giving up was both tiring and soothing enough to delay its fulfilment. When passion failed to keep me here, paralysis would work just as well.

I walked past another collapsible colony of benders, avoiding the charred patches of ground left by former fires.

'Better go back,' I thought without acting on it. I was constantly overhearing dull internal mandates. I tried to avoid seeing the fence and the soldiers to my right, the mansions to my left. Nothing to look at but the spiny grass. A phenomenon of limited fascination. Some men had offered to run a play group for children during the action. I spotted their camp near a wooded area shielded from the road. I decided to wander over to have a look at their playbus.

Suddenly I stopped dead. Paul.

No, it cannot be you. It cannot be.

A moment's dizziness, a reluctance to meet the past. But it was Paul. Of course! He would come here. It was logical. I looked away, checked again. So near to him, I could see the steam of his breath, hear him sigh as he crouched to stick a tent peg into the ground. Crooked white scar tracking down his left temple to the eye. Emphasised now by a tan. How did he get a winter tan?

A furious sexual tenderness went through me at the memory of stroking and kissing that scar. Artwork executed by some childhood enemy with a well-aimed stone. He still had that stupid little beard, adding severity to his El Greco face. Brown eyes sad as ever, the mouth pinched and mean even in repose. And yet he was more beautiful than before. In a rough and different way, as if beauty had been beaten into him.

How dare you come here? A gate-crashing ghost.

'Walk away, walk away,' the monitor in my head nagged. But I stood rooted to the earth. Afraid to flout the mysterious inescapable magnetism that had brought us both together to this spot in time and space. Paul stopped work and blew his nose with a loud snort, diminishing his own resurrected splendour. Reminding me at the same time of the shaming fits of physical intolerance that had bedevilled our marriage.

'He hated you! He couldn't stand you!' I was telling myself when he cast a glance in my direction. I turned to make my getaway.

'Hey! Hey! Stop!'

His feet behind me, his breathing. He overtook me.

'It *is* you.'

'Hello, Paul.'

'It was when you shrugged that I . . .'

We stood there in a trance of embarrassment. 'You've cut your hair.'

'It's more convenient. For here.'

He was inspecting me avidly. I was angry at not looking my 'best' and angry for caring.

'You're living here, then?'

'Some of the time.'

'What's it like?'

'Hard.'

He stared, expecting more details.

'There's a lot of hostility. Not that I care what anyone thinks of me! Not any more.'

'How've you been?' he asked. His voice was hoarse.

'Fine. You?'

'Fine.'

He grimaced. 'That's what everybody says. Fine. Fine.'

'It's the easiest thing to say.'

'And to hear.'

'I have a daughter,' I said it like a formal announcement.

'Ah . . . A daughter! That's good. That's wonderful. And a father, I suppose. I mean, she has . . . You have someone?'

'She's two years old.'

'You look frozen. Let me give you some real coffee,' he offered.

'No. Thanks.'

'Yes, go on. I do a really good cup of coffee now!'

'So what else is new?'

He laughed but a look of pain crossed his face. 'I don't know.'

We tramped back the short way to the camp in silence. The sound of the wind keening in the guy ropes made me shiver.

'Where's everyone?'

'Gathering wood.'

From the bus he fetched two canvas chairs and then a steaming jug of coffee which he poured into plastic cups.

'Oh, a real chair!'

'All mod. cons.'

'How did you get involved in this sort of thing? Providing a crêche?' I sounded like a polite interviewer.

'I'm a play group organiser. It's my profession now.'

154

'It's only a profession when a man does it!' I tried to joke but it came out sour.

'Well, childcare is badly undervalued. So are children.'

'But not by you? Something has changed, then.' A conversation stopper. I forced the black bitter liquid down my throat. Faint sounds of clowning, chatter, wild laughter reached us from a distance. I poured the dregs of the coffee onto the flames, making an angry hissing noise.

' "We have nothing to say to each other",' I quoted. He stared into the fire, frowning and mute, as if he had forgotten my presence. 'It seems you were right! Though I didn't think so at the time. I had a million things to say to you. When I read your farewell note, I couldn't believe you truly thought there was nothing left to say!' I laughed. ' "We have nothing to say to each other," "No other way," "I'm doing this for both our sakes." Such trite expressions! From someone with your dazzling education, I would have expected a more stylish epitaph for our marriage!'

'So treachery is acceptable if it's done with literary finesse?'

'No, treachery is not acceptable!'

No response. Just like old times. And I was starting to feel the same nervous irritated desire for him. Or was it the same nervous irritated lack of desire? I spoke again: 'After you left, I kept talking to you. I couldn't stop. It was so quiet in the house. The silence magnified every little noise. Even the daylight seemed to have a sound.'

I stood up.

'Where are you going?'

'I don't want to get into an action replay of how things used to be. The Way We Were! Me baring my soul, while you sit there like a Martian!'

'I could never compete!'

'What?'

'With you lining up your feelings. You and your fancy words!'

'Silence is a weapon too.'

'Sometimes it's a cover for confusion. I just didn't know what to say to you.'

'So you disappeared! What a revenge!'

'It wasn't to punish you.'

'How could I be free after that?'

He shrugged. 'I was no good for you. I hoped you would find someone else.'

'I found plenty. Plenty of takers. And fakers.'

'No one special?'

'That's what my father always asks! "Any men in your life?" "Fixed up yet?" As if I'm some kind of vacancy!'

'He must have been glad when we split.'

'When *you* split! He was overjoyed. "Didn't I warn you never to trust a Catholic? They always stab you in the back!" That's what he said.'

'You only married me to get at your parents. Rich Protestant princess slumming with a croppy boy!'

'It was just you and me, Paul! Just you and me!'

'You could have outdone any Catholic in hatred of Protestants. You'd had it up to the gills with "hymns and hypocrisy", quote unquote.'

'And injustice!'

'That's my girl! The champion of the underdog. But you envied us underdogs, didn't you? Our Culture! You were sick of being the Brits' country cousin, trying to feel that Tennyson and Wordsworth and the Wars of the Roses were really part of your heritage. And so we had the 'Teach Yourself Irish', the rebel plaints played at full volume, the trips to Dublin to breathe the "pure heady air." You steeped yourself in the history and the culture and the kitsch . . .'

'Who's full of the fancy words now?'

'It's my turn!'

'Why didn't you take your bloody turn then? Why did you have to destroy everything?'

'Destroy what? Your fantasy? A Republican husband was just another ingredient in your romance. Part of the refurbishment of your image!'

'No! No!'

'You even managed to envy my stinking childhood! How you would have enjoyed the handmedowns, the leaky shoes, the glorious pain of neglected teeth! You thought you were hard done by with all those big comfortable rooms as backdrop to your martyrdom. With your weird mama and her well-therapized anguish. You thought my mother was a 'real mum'. Jesus! She was a slave! When she was thirty-five, she looked fifty. Nine kids. That bloody awful helpless fecundity. Every eighteen months a new head to be counted. Another gob to be stuffed with chips and jam sandwiches. Three of us to each bed. God, the tunrnipy smell of the sheets in the mornings, that's what I remember!

And hearing my parents at it behind the wall. Him plugging her. It always sounded like a criminal act. I hate it when I see her expression on other women. That dazed bestial self-immolation.'

'You detest women,' I accused him. 'I remember the way you used to say "cunt". With such venom. It was your favourite term of abuse for people you disliked.'

'Aw, leave out the Puffin psychology!'

'You say you hated what your mother became. But all you wanted was a woman who would be a comfort station. The spiritual equivalent of an inflatable doll!'

'There's no shortage!'

'Hypocrite! You hate women but you come here pretending to support us! You moan about your childhood but Jesus, you loved it! I've heard you so many times listing every sacred grievance, you never leave any items out, you revel in the pain of it! You and your loveless childhood and your loveless marriage! Damn you, I loved you! I loved every bone in your stupid body!'

'Especially one.'

'O God! Now we're getting to it. Out of your own mouth . . .'

'You look very triumphant.'

'You were so screwed up about sex. You made me ashamed of my desire. Of my . . . myself.'

'I'm sorry.'

'What?'

'I'm sorry. My sex education was more effective than yours, that's all.'

'You were too pure for me.'

'Quite the opposite.'

'What do you mean?'

'Nothing.'

The talking fizzled out. With an effort I started up again. 'Paul? I remember once we were talking and you said that the worst thing about separation from someone you loved . . . from someone important . . . was not the loss of their presence but not knowing what was happening to them. Their absence became a space filled with fear.'

He sighed. 'I know what you're asking, I know . . . But what good can come from this? We're like two people who've died and met in Hell to rake over the past. I wish . . .'

'Paul, I need to understand. You've got to set me free. The baby . . .'

'Your girl?'

'No. Our baby.'

He stood up and started to pace back and forth, hugging himself as if to keep warm.

'We didn't have a baby. That was a seven week foetus. A lump of overgrown sperm.' /

'You were so desperate for me to get rid of it. But afterwards, I think you blamed me. That's when things really started to go wrong,' I stated, wanting simplicity.

'Ha! Short memory! That's what you want to think. The slaughter of innocence ruined our marriage. Eh? We killed an unborn child and our "love" at the same time?' He put on a voice like a commercial for a soppy film: ' "Hands that never grew prised them apart!" No, the death of innocence happened before that.'

'What do you mean?'

He kneeled and started loading twigs onto the fire. 'Remember when two of my workmates were murdered within a fortnight of each other?'

'Yes. I remember their funerals. I remember you sleeping with the light on for weeks afterwards.'

'They were both Catholics, no paramilitary connections, both tortured and killed in the same way. All the Catholics on the payroll, there were only six of us, were scared shitless. We wondered if somebody in work had it in for us. We wondered who would be next. Well, there was this big Prod, McCready, not too much up top, all bulk and bravado. Reserve cop. Couldn't wait to get into the old lovat green uniform every weekend. At first, I thought no, it couldn't be him. He was an amiable savage, mean . . . but not grisly. But then I thought he wouldn't have to do the job himself, he could just tip the wink to . . . whoever. And then I heard him defend the assassination gangs. He compared them to the French Resistance fighters! He said they never carried out random murders, they always knew something. "No smoke without fire." Their targets were always Provos, no mistake about it. They only exterminated vermin. Brought people to "justice" who would otherwise escape. They were a useful adjunct to the law.'

'Christ!'

'I suspected him more and more. He was in a position to know the movements and the addresses of the dead men. He was the common factor.'

'But it could have been anyone, Paul! Nobody could be trusted.'

'I know, I know. But I convinced myself it was him. You see, if it was him, I didn't have to fear everybody else! The word got out. The Provos decided to get him.'

'Well then, they must have found out that he was the culprit.'

'Oh, not necessarily. He was a part-time cop; that would be enough reason for them. You must remember how they like to cull the police force. Anyway, they killed his brother by mistake. Same house, same haircut. He was the one who answered the bloody door.'

'Jesus, they got the wrong man!'

'But don't you see, even the "right" man might have been the wrong man!' He started to cry. 'I'm the one who put the word out! . . .No, don't touch me! Don't you understand that I'm exactly the same as the man who condemned my two friends?'

'Yes,' I whispered.

'I tried to confess to the priest, but I couldn't. Couldn't tell you. I went to that psychiatrist, not to tell him, just to see him, just to know that he was there . . . But it was no use . . . I went home and swallowed the whole bottle of pills he prescribed . . .'

'He put you in that terrible place.'

'I was glad.'

'To be cooped up with all those despairing and deranged people?'

He laughed. 'Sounds more like the Outside . . . I needed the break. There were schizos in there who smeared themselves and their bed linen and the walls with excrement. Not to announce their smelly rage or anything like that. To them shit was just a neutral bodily substance, a handy medium.'

'How do you know that, Paul?'

He ignored me. 'It was the time of the dirt protest, remember. You were involved in the campaign of support for the prisoners. "They're enraged to the very bowels" you said. Suddenly shit was heroic. And I realised I was sick of all those hierarchies of value, you know, the arse is inferior to the eye, especially the Third Eye, porridge is inferior to poetry, and so on. Madness was such a holiday from all that. I wanted nothing more to do with all those tables of values and systems of salvation that lead to murder! That's why I had to get away from Ireland.

'But it was too late. I was cold and brutal. I cursed myself when I instigated that murder. I couldn't have a child . . .'

Suddenly I understood. 'Or a wife?'

'Or a wife.'

I thought of the policeman's dead brother, of my lonely tormented husband, the strange malevolent chain of fear and suspicion and circumstance that had linked them forever.

'But don't I exist? Don't I?' The protest flared and died in silence.

'What will happen to you?' I said.

'Nothing. I just look after children, work for peace. I try to do no more harm. That's more ambitious than it sounds! But look at you, I've made you miserable.' He laughed. 'The Way We Were! . . . Fran?' It was the first time he had spoken my name.

'Yes?'

'I loved you as much as I could.'

'Yes.'

We held each other for a long moment before I rose and without another word walked back to the women.